FIRE IN THE NIGHT

Fargo was dead asleep when it happened. Now it looked like he was going to be simply dead.

The farmhouse where he was sleeping was on fire. Smoke was filling up the last bit of air he could breathe. Skye grabbed a sheet, whipped it around himself, and ran through the fire. Calling on all the strength in his leg muscles, he leaped head first through the window and the wall of flames engulfing the building.

He hit the ground, the sheet around him ablaze. He rolled free of it and swept the scene with angry eyes. He heard hoofbeats receding in the night and raced to his Ovaro. Galloping after the attackers, he found five horsemen moving casually down a hill in the moonlight, confident they had done their job. They started to glance back as he charged down at them, but he had his Colt in his hand.

"Surprise, you bastards," he shouted as he fired.

MOON LAKE MASSACRE

by

Jon Sharpe

A SIGNET BOOK

SIGNET
Published by the Penguin Group
Penguin Books USA Inc., 375 Hudson Street,
New York, New York 10014, U.S.A.
Penguin Books Ltd, 27 Wrights Lane,
London W8 5TZ, England
Penguin Books Australia Ltd, Ringwood,
Victoria, Australia
Penguin Books Canada Ltd, 10 Alcorn Avenue,
Toronto, Ontario, Canada M4V 3B2
Penguin Books (N.Z.) Ltd, 182-190 Wairau Road,
Auckland 10, New Zealand

Penguin Books Ltd, Registered Offices:
Harmondsworth, Middlesex, England

First published by Signet,
an imprint of New American Library,
a division of Penguin Books USA Inc.

First Printing, May, 1993
10 9 8 7 6 5 4 3 2 1

The first chapter of this book previously appeared in *Texas Triggers*, the one hundred thirty-sixth volume in this series.

REGISTERED TRADEMARK—MARCA REGISTRADA

Printed in the United States of America

The Trailsman

Beginnings . . . they bend the tree and they mark the man. Skye Fargo was born when he was eighteen. Terror was his midwife, vengeance his first cry. Killing spawned Skye Fargo, ruthless, cold-blooded murder. Out of the acrid smoke of gunpowder still hanging in the air, he rose, cried out a promise never forgotten.

The Trailsman they began to call him all across the West: searcher, scout, hunter, the man who could see where others only looked, his skills for hire but not his soul, the man who lived each day to the fullest, yet trailed each tomorrow. Skye Fargo, the Trailsman, the seeker who could take the wildness of a land and the wanting of a woman and make them his own.

1860, Utah—land of
saints and sinners where some
tried to build the future
on greed and killing . . .

1

They were still shadowing him. The big man astride the magnificent Ovaro let his lake blue eyes squint into the setting sun. The six riders had been trailing him most of the day, staying well back in the bur oak and shadbush. But he had spotted the slender shape of bows slung across the shoulders of two of the riders, and he'd caught the glint of sun on red-brown torsos. This was the Utah Territory, mostly Ute country, though sometimes the Arapaho ventured into it. It was a land that in some places was rich and green and in others dry and parched. Happily, he rode through the rich, green terrain of low hills well-covered with good shade trees.

The six riders bothered him but not simply because they'd been trailing him. It was how they were doing it that nagged at him. It wasn't normal for six braves to trail their quarry most of the day. There had been plenty of places they could have come at him, numerous spots where he'd been ready and waiting, expecting an attack. But none had come. They had continued to hang back, seemingly content to just trail him. It was almost as if they waited to see where he was going. Very strange indeed, he frowned to himself as the sun began to drop over the distant hills. The blackness of night would quickly descend, he knew, and he found a spot to bed down under the tapering leaves of a bur oak.

Skye Fargo decided to leave the saddle on the horse, just in case, and as night enveloped the land he made a small fire. He set his bedroll beside the fire and stretched out to heat some beef strips from his saddlebag.

They were still in the trees, watching. They hadn't gone their way. He felt it, knew it. But they were too far away to see much but the shape of him in the glow of the small fire. As he slowly chewed the beef strips, he again wondered why six braves had wasted a day shadowing him. Was it merely a harbinger of stranger things to come? The letter in his pocket had certainly hinted at devious turns. Perhaps the actions of the six Indians was simply a reflection of the spirit of this Utah territory, a land where those who professed themselves saints and those who plainly were sinners staked their respective claims. In this land perhaps God and the devil were both bystanders.

Yet he had come, drawn by old memories and old loyalties, and he took the letter from his pocket and read it again by the fire's light.

Dear Skye Fargo,

I am writing on account of an old friend of yours, Ben Adams. He needs help but he is too stubborn and too proud to ask for it. He has often talked about you and so I am writing this to you. He'd be real mad at me if he knew.

As Ben's friend, I know he is afraid and into more than he can handle and I am afraid for him. I don't want to put him in any more danger than he is now so I won't meet you here at Moon Lake. But there's a village named Duchess nearby in the north Utah Territory.

I'll got there on July 6th and stay at the Inn for three days I hope you can meet me there for Ben's sake. He's told me you ride a fine Ovaro so I'll know you when you arrive.

After you cross the White River and go over the hills, find an old ox trail. Take it north and it'll lead you right into Duchess. Thank you.

Ellie Willis

Fargo folded the letter back into his pocket. Ben Adams had been a good friend of his father's, a real friend who stood by his pa when the times were hardest. Fargo always wanted to find a way to repay Ben Adams, but in time the man had moved away and the debt was still unpaid. Maybe this was the chance, at last. Ben had written him a few times over the years, reaching him care of General Delivery at the Springfield Post Depot, just where this letter had finally reached him.

He had taken off at once, realizing July sixth wasn't that far away. But he'd made good time and he expected he'd be reaching Duchess by tomorrow, only a day late. The letter had evoked old memories, but it had raised more questions than answers and he looked forward to meeting Ellie Willis. He let the small fire go out and sat in the inky blackness for a moment, then slid from the bedroll. He took a blanket, wrapped it around himself and sank into the nearby brush. The Colt in his hand, he let himself sleep, certain he'd hear any attack on the bedroll.

But the night passed quietly and he woke with the dawn sun, used his canteen to wash, and breakfasted on a stand of wild blackberry. He surveyed the land as he rolled up his bedroll and only the flash of a Bullock's oriole broke the calm with a brief explosion of orange and black. He unsaddled the Ovaro and used a body brush from his knapsack to go over the horse's coat with a quick grooming. When he saddled up again, he headed the horse downward through the hills, the sun glistening on the jet black fore and hind quarters and pure white midsection. He rode slowly, making no direct glances but letting himself scan the tree cover to his rear, and finally he spotted the silent forms again trailing him and again staying back.

He frowned as he rode. What were they waiting for, he asked himself again. It was not usual Indian behavior simply to follow, so he purposely made his way through a narrow passage, the Colt in his hand, waiting for them to attack. But no attack came in the perfect place for one, and he emerged and rode up the side of the next low hill. The white river was long behind him, and he saw the last of the hills loom up ahead as he rode on with the sun moving into midafternoon. The silent riders still followed, still stayed in the trees when he moved down out of the last of the low hills.

Three trails furrowed the land, one far too narrow, the second one heading over a series of rocky mounds no ox-drawn wagons would have taken, and the third plainly the old ox trail, wide enough for wagons and flat enough for oxen. He paused for a long moment as he surveyed the three trails and then turned the pinto down the ox trail. His glance went to both sides of the trail where thick growths of box elder rose up, and he cast a glance behind him as he rode. The gray-purple haze of dusk had begun to filter down when he spotted the movement in the trees, no longer to his rear but in the foliage alongside the road. Their stalking and trailing was over, Fargo knew, and he drew the Colt at the same time as he dug his heels into the Ovaro's ribs.

The horse leaped forward into an instant gallop, and Fargo half turned in the saddle, the Colt upraised, waiting for the Indians to come out of the trees and onto the road. He was confident of picking off at least two as they came into the open but, as he frowned in surprise, they stayed in the tree cover, and he saw the arrows rushing toward him. They were wild, and Fargo kept the horse running forward as he glanced into the trees where the Indians remained and the dusk grew deeper. He didn't understand any of it. They couldn't ride fast enough to keep up with him if they stayed in the trees and yet they did, and he saw another cluster of arrows fly his way, again off the mark.

But suddenly he heard the sound of rifle fire, and he turned, ducking low as two shots came close. Staying low in the saddle, he swerved the horse as another pair of shots resounded. As he steered the Ovaro toward the trees at his right, he saw another four arrows hurtle through the air toward him. He raced into the trees, yanked the horse to a stop, and aimed the Colt at the three horsemen charging him. His first two shots missed as his targets were mostly hidden in the foliage, but he heard a grunt of pain as his third shot connected. He waited, Colt ready to fire. The three riders turned, half hidden in the trees as they raced away.

Fargo heard the hooves at his left and saw the three near-naked riders crossing the road toward him, one with a rifle he fired into the trees, spraying shots in a wide pattern. Fargo dropped from the saddle as the bullets slammed into the branches at his back. He returned fire on one knee, and again the attackers peeled away and ran. The first three were already out of sight in the gray dimness of dusk, and Fargo leaped onto the Ovaro and sent the horse racing down to the road where the other three Indians were fleeing. They were starting to turn back into the trees when he took aim, fired, and saw one topple from his horse. The other two raced on, not pausing, and Fargo reined to a halt and heard the sound of hoofbeats moving away through the trees.

He stayed in place, waited, still listening, and his eyes peered into the box elder at the other side of the road. Nothing moved and the only sound was the hoofbeats fading away. He took the moment to reload, a frown digging into his brow. It had been unlike any Indian attack he'd ever seen, almost inept, certainly without the reckless ferocity of most Indian attacks. Nothing about their actions had been in character, and his glance went to the arrows littering the road. He bent down and picked up four of the shafts. Two held Ute markings and two were crudely made and unmarked. He moved on and picked up three more. The first two held Ute markings on their shafts; the third was also unmarked.

Fargo's frown deepened as he stared down at the hoofprints in the soil. None were the unshod prints of Indian ponies, every mark made by a horseshoed hoof. His lips in a grimace, he strode forward to the motionless figure a half dozen yards away. The man wore only a loincloth and lay on his face, his long black hair falling in disarray over his head. Fargo's bullet had penetrated the base of his neck, and a line of red spilled down his back. As he peered down, Fargo saw that the man's skin alongside the blood had seemed to turn pale where the red liquid washed down his body. Fargo dropped to one knee, wet his finger with his lips, and ran it down the side of the man's torso. He lifted the finger to stare at the red-brown smudge on the tip.

"Dye," he murmured aloud, the reddish brown tone the probable product of crushed juniper berries and henna. He rose, used the top of his boot to turn the body over, and the long black hair fell from the man's head to lay on the ground beside him. His face had also been dyed, but his hair was close-cropped under where the wig had been. No Indians, none of them, Fargo muttered to himself as he returned to the Ovaro and their strange actions had been explained. But nothing else, and as he climbed onto the saddle and the night descended, he began to put together what had happened.

Questions and answers pushed at each other. Why had they trailed him for days? There had to be only one answer. They weren't certain he was the one they wanted. They plainly knew the man they wanted rode an Ovaro, and while Ovaros weren't commonplace, his wasn't the only one. They wanted to be sure and only when they saw him turn onto the old ox trail to Duchess were they certain he was the one they wanted. The Indian disguise was simple enough to explain. Someone wanted him to appear to have been killed by Indian arrows. There was always the chance that the attack might be seen so the elaborate disguise was needed.

Only, to their surprise, he had been ready for them. They were quick to break off the attack rather than have their masquerade exposed.

But the one attacker he'd brought down had done exactly that, and Fargo's thoughts continued to probe. Someone didn't want him to meet with Ellie Willis, and that someone knew Ellie had sent for him. Suddenly Ellie Willis was a very key figure, source of all the questions needing answers, and he put the Ovaro into a trot as the half moon rose. When he reached the town of Duchess, the half light revealed nothing extraordinary: it was a double row of ramshackle houses with the main street running between them. The town saloon sent a square of light into the street when he passed, and he pulled to a halt some fifty yards on before a white clapboard, two-story building. Two lamps flanked the door and lighted a sign that read DUCHESS INN. He tethered the horse at the hitching post and strode into the building where a bald-headed man in shirtsleeves sat behind a front desk.

" 'Evening," the man said and nodded.

"You've an Ellie Willis registered here?" Fargo asked.

The clerk had no need to check his desk register, an indication that they weren't exactly chock-full with boarders. "Room four, end of hall on ground floor," he said.

Fargo nodded and found his way down the wide hallway to the last door. It was opened at his knock, and he felt a moment of surprise at the young woman who faced him, a round, pretty face with tightly curled blond hair and a wide mouth with full, sensuous lips. Ample breasts pushed out a dark green blouse, and a black cotton skirt flowed over hips that curved nicely into long thighs.

"Skye Fargo," he said, and she studied his face, a tiny furrow touching her smooth forehead.

"Your horse outside?" she asked and he nodded. She closed the door and strode down the hall and he followed. She stepped out of the inn and halted before the pinto, taking the horse in with a long glance. "All right," she said, turning to him. "Let's go back inside." Once again he followed her and she admitted him to the room, modest with a single bed and small dresser to one side. A stuffed chair and an end table completed the furnishings. "Can't be too careful," she said. "Besides, I wasn't sure you'd come." She paused and her eyes studied him again. "You seemed surprised when you saw me just now."

"Guess so," he admitted. 'Somehow, I expected an older woman. You're much younger than I thought you'd be."

"Why'd you expect an older woman?" she asked.

"I'm not exactly sure of that. Maybe because Ben Adams is getting on, and you wrote that you were a friend of his," Fargo said.

"So you'd expect he'd have an older woman as a friend." Ellie Willis half smiled.

"More or less," Fargo admitted. "But then, the day's been full of surprises."

"Such as?" Ellie Willis asked.

"A passel of fake Indians tried to do me in," Fargo said.

"Fake Indians?" She frowned.

"That's right. I figure it has to be connected with whatever trouble Ben's got himself into," Fargo said. "Maybe you'd best start giving me the details on that."

"I can't, really," Ellie Willis said, and it was Fargo's turn to be surprised. She sat down on the edge of the bed and gave a small shrug of helplessness. "What I mean is that he never really told me anything."

"You just knew he was in trouble?" Fargo queried.

"Yes, by the way he was acting. But there's more. Whatever it is, or was, he's gone from it," she said.

Fargo felt irritation joining surprise. "What's that mean?" He frowned.

"Ben took up and left," she said. "Two weeks ago."

"Just like that? No reasons? No explanations?"

"None. Didn't even say if he'd be back. It was too late for me to get hold of you, so I came to keep our meeting," Ellie Willis said and rose to stand before him. Her hand came up to rest against his chest, and her eyes were round and full of apology. "I'm sorry. There just was no way for me to reach you. I feel terrible about this."

"I'm not too happy about it, either, honey," Fargo admitted crossly, and then softened his words as she seemed sincerely contrite. "But I guess you're not to blame. As you said, it was too late to reach me."

Her hand tightened on his arm. "Thanks for understanding. You're as nice as Ben said you were. But I feel it is my fault. If I hadn't gone and written you, you'd not have come all this way. I'd like to make it up to you," she said.

"Don't see how you could do that," Fargo said blandly.

"By finding out if something else Ben said about you was right," Ellie murmured.

"What was that?"

"He said you were quite a man with the ladies," she said, her full lips turning into a wide smile. "I'd like to find out. It would make me feel better about my bringing you all this way for nothing."

"Just that?"

"No, not just that. You're too damn good-looking to just let pass by," Ellie Willis said. "How's that for honesty?"

"Good enough," Fargo said, and her arms slid around his neck and her wide, sensuous lips found his. She pressed and opened her lips. He felt her tongue darting out, drawing back, sliding out again, and the warm hunger of her was very real. He still had a lot of questions to ask but they could wait. Pleasure before business. He always preferred that to the usual way, and he went with her as she fell back onto the bed.

His hands undid buttons and the dark green blouse came off, her camisole top slipping down, and he saw modest but very round breasts, surprisingly pale white with very dark red nipples and dark circles around each. He pulled off clothes as she slid from her skirt, and he saw wide hips, a little layer of extra flesh over them, a rounded belly and a modest little triangle that narrowed down to full thighs, also with an extra few pounds on them.

His hand encased one pale white breast, and it was very soft, flattening at his touch. He put his mouth down to the dark red nipple and drew it in gently. Ellie Willis gave a sharp cry of delight.

"Yes, oh, Jeeez, yes," she said and pushed upward. He took in more of the soft, pale white mound. She half turned, brought the other breast to him, and he took it, passing from one to the other as she cried out with each touch and her hands moved slowly up and down his chest. Her tongue licked against the side of his face, and her sharp cries turned to eager moaning when her hand reached down and touched his throbbing maleness. Her body shuddered, drew back, and thrust upward. "Oh, God, please, please," she murmured, and he saw her fleshy thighs falling open, twisting, closing, opening again.

He came to her and paused, feeling the moistness of her open portal. He rested there for a moment as she half screamed and pushed her torso upward at him, and then he slid forward into the dark warm tunnel. "Oh, God, yes, yes . . . oh, oh yes," Ellie Willis moaned and moved with him, calling out with his every slow thrust. Her hands dug into his back, and her curved little belly jiggled as she pushed and lifted with her hips. Her thighs were clasped around him, pressing hard, squeezing as if in echo of his thrusts inside her. For all her eager delights, she managed to pace herself, and he drew in the wonderful pleasure of her wet warmth, soothing and exciting all at once, her very real wanting adding another dimension to their pleasure.

She had turned out to be a complete suprise, but then the unexpected things were often the best. Her arms pulled his head down into her soft breasts and held him there as her hips twisted and rose with him and her gasps grew harsher. He felt himself gathering, spiraling, and suddenly her warm walls contracted around him. A scream rose from her, and she stiffened against him, suspended, embracing and embraced by that all-encompassing climax. He exploded with her and heard his own cry of ecstasy that was both release and despair, a forever moment. He sank down with her as she fell back onto the bed, but her thighs stayed around him, holding him inside her.

"Oh, God, oh God," Ellie Willis murmured, and his face pressed into her soft breasts and stayed there. He enjoyed the touch of her, surrounding and enveloping. Finally her thighs fell open, and he slid from her to lay at her side. After a moment she turned to him, her dark red nipples pressed against his chest. "That was something special," she said.

"I'm glad," he replied.

"I feel better now, about everything," Ellie remarked.

"Good. I wouldn't want your conscience hurting on my account," Fargo said.

"It would have," she said.

"Where is Moon Lake?" he asked.

"About ten miles west."

"You and Ben live there?" he questioned.

"No, I live in town. So did Ben. It's only a few miles from Moon Lake. They call it Moonside," Ellie told him.

"What did Ben do there?"

"He worked for a big rancher whose spread is near Moon Lake."

"And you?"

"I work in a store in town.'

"What kind of a store?" Fargo asked.

She frowned at him and rose on one elbow. "Why all the questions?" she asked.

"I'm just naturally curious. You don't seem like the shopgirl type," Fargo said.

"Ladies' wear," Ellie said and folded herself against him, her soft breasts flattening onto his chest. "Stay awhile, tomorrow and tomorrow night. I'd like that. I don't have to get back for another day."

"More conscience? Not that I could object to an offer like that," he added hastily.

"No, no more conscience. This is just for me. I haven't had a man in a long time, and I've never had one like you," she said. "Please?"

He shrugged. "I've nowhere to go except back," he said, and she smiled, her wide mouth closed over his. Before she went to sleep in his arms she showed him again how appreciative she was.

He slept contentedly late into the morning, and Ellie Willis woke as he did. He watched her use the washbasin. Her figure seemed more ample than it had during the night, little creases of extra flesh around her belly and thighs. But she definitely had an earthy sensuousness about her, and he was sorry to see her slip the brown dress on.

"I'll go out and wait for you. I understand they serve a good breakfast here," she said.

"All right. Then I've a horse to tend to," he told her.

"Let's spend the day doing nothing. We can look through town and relax together. I haven't had a day doing nothing in a long time," Ellie said wistfully.

"It's a deal," he said, and she hurried from the room. She was seated at a table in the dining room when he came out, biscuits and coffee waiting, and he realized he was hungry. She made small talk through breakfast and went with him when he took the Ovaro to the public stable, unsaddled the horse, and paid for a roomy stall. Later she strolled through town with him, investigated the merchandise at the general store, and paused to read the schedule at the stage depot. "How'd you come here?" he asked

"A friend drove me. She's coming to get me tomorrow," Ellie said as she strolled on with him, her arm linked in his, a sweet warmth to her. Outside of town they found a small stream and stretched out in the sun. "What will you do when you get back?" she asked.

"Find two or three jobs waiting for me. There usually are," he said. "You going to stay in Moonside and see if Ben comes back?"

"Yes," she said.

"Write me if he does. I'm just curious," Fargo said.

"If you like." She nodded and lay hard against him, and they watched the sun go down. When they returned to town, they ate in the dining room at the inn—corn fritters and chicken legs—and afterward, back in her room, she came to him with all the hungry wanting of the night before. The night grew deep before he slept, satiated with pleasant exhaustion. The trip hadn't turned out as he thought it would, he told himself, but it certainly hadn't been a waste of time. The pleasure of that thought added to the contentment of his deep sleep.

Once again he indulged himself and slept into the morning, and when he woke he felt for her warmth beside him. But his wandering hand found only empty air as he sat up. He was alone in the room as well as in the bed. Her clothes were also gone, he saw. She must have very carefully slipped from the bed while he was still deep in sleep. She had to have been quiet for him not to have felt her leave. He rose, washed, and strode from the room. The desk clerk looked up as he halted before him. "The young lady from room four, you see her this morning?" Fargo asked.

"Yes, she left," the clerk said. "Left a note for you." He handed Fargo a small square of paper that Fargo unfolded to scan the few lines:

> It's best this way. I don't trust myself facing you come morning. Have a good trip back . . . Ellie.

He scowled as he stuffed the note into his pocket and walked from the inn. At the stable he paid the night's bill and saddled the Ovaro to ride out of town. But the scowl stayed on his face. Something didn't fit. Or, perhaps more accurately, something new didn't fit. Suddenly Ellie's behavior seemed as strange as the fake Indians who had tried to kill him. A stab of uneasiness speared him, and a new set of questions churned in his mind.

He had believed her about Ben suddenly running off and how sorry she'd been for bringing him all this way for nothing. God knows she'd proved how contrite she'd been. With that kind of proof he'd no reason to disbelieve her. But now, her vanishing in the night simply didn't fit. It was plain that she had sent for him. Had somebody changed her friendship and concern for Ben Adams? Had she really come to turn him around?

Something didn't set right at all, and Fargo turned the Ovaro west. Ellie Willis had some more questions to answer.

2

As Fargo neared the town, he saw Moon Lake in the distance, a large and brilliant blue circle as the sun glinted on its surface. The town itself proved to be more ordinary than most, small and rambling with a collection of wood and clapboard buildings. Fargo moved slowly down the main street, his eyes taking in a barber shop, a blacksmith, a half dozen warehouse sheds, a saloon, and a feed store. No "ladies' wear store." He frowned. There *was* an open-faced trading store that served as a general store. He came to a white-bearded man whittling atop a tall water barrel, who looked as though he'd know everyone and everything in town.

"Howdy," Fargo said as he halted. "I'm looking for someone. Ellie Willis. Would you know where I might find her?"

The old man paused in his whittling to squint up at Fargo and took a moment before answering. "Ellie Willis?" he echoed, and Fargo nodded. "You'd best go see Doc Elton," the man said. "Last house in town, white fence out front."

"Obliged," Fargo said and moved the pinto forward, conscious of the man's eyes following him. The doctor's house was easy enough to find, the white fence fronting a modest house with a larger section built onto the rear. The small sign caught his eye: DOC ELTON - OFFICE AND SANATORIUM.

Fargo dismounted and knocked on the door. The figure that answered wore a black vest over a white shirt, a tall, gangling figure, slightly stooped with graying hair atop a long, doleful face. But behind steel-rimmed spectacles a pair of blue eyes seemed both kindly and sharp.

"Doc Elton?" Fargo ventured.

"It is," the man said.

"Name's Fargo . . . Skye Fargo. I'm looking for Ellie Willis. I was told to come see you," the Trailsman said.

Doc Elton's face took on a quizzical stare. "You a friend of Ellie's?" he asked.

"Sort of," Fargo answered.

"I'm sorry. You're a day late. Ellie died yesterday," the doctor said.

Fargo's mouth came open as he stared back. "No, that can't be," he breathed.

"I'm afraid it is, friend," Doc Elton said. "Would you like to see her? She's laid out down at Ed Brumby's. Ed's our undertaker."

"Yes, I sure would," Fargo said.

"I'll take you. It's a short walk." Doc led the way down the street to a low-roofed building with one window along the side. Fargo followed Doc Elton inside and immediately saw the open pine casket in the center of the floor. Fargo walked to it, Doc Elton beside him, and he stared down at the body inside—a woman in a plain blue dress, gray hair, and a face lined but pleasant, a woman of some fifty years of age, he guessed.

"That's Ellie Willis?" Fargo muttered.

"Of course," Doc Elton said, and Fargo looked

up to see the doctor glaring at him. "I thought you said you were a friend of hers."

"I thought I was," Fargo said. Something was very wrong, he added silently as the doctor's eyes probed his.

"You're not making much sense, Fargo," Doc Elton said.

"Neither is this," Fargo snapped. "You've a sheriff here?"

"No. If we need a sheriff, we call Bill Staley in Duchess. Why do you ask that?" Doc said.

Fargo gestured to the casket. "What happened to her?"

Doc Elton's lips pursed. "I don't rightly know. It was all very strange. Ellie's never been sick a day in her life, and she suddenly collapsed a little over a week ago. She went into a coma, could hardly breathe. I did everything I could for her, but nothing helped. Poor Ellie. She fought though, hung on as long as she could."

"She say anything?"

"Once, when she came out of the coma for a few moments. 'He's coming. I have to wait. I have to wait,' she said. It didn't make any sense to me."

"It makes sense to me. She was waiting for me to arrive," Fargo said grimly. He understood Doc Elton's stare of incomprehension. Nothing was making much sense to him, either. He needed more information. He had to trust somebody, and Doc had a basic honesty in his face. Reading a man's face was not so different from reading a trail, and he'd had plenty of experience at both. "Can we talk somewhere?" he asked.

"My place," the doctor said, and Fargo followed back to the house where he was led into a small but neat office—a stethoscope on the desk and medical books on the shelves. He lowered himself into a chair as the doctor sat down behind the desk.

"One more question before I talk. What can you tell me about Ben Adams running away?" Fargo asked.

"Ben Adams didn't run away," the doctor said. "He was killed a few weeks ago, a freak accident."

"The little bitch," Fargo muttered.

"What?" Doc frowned.

"Later," Fargo said. "Killed in a freak accident? What kind of accident?" he asked as he inwardly cursed a wide, sensuous mouth and tightly curled blond hair.

"It seems his horse threw him, and he broke his neck," the doctor said.

"Anybody see it happen?" Fargo questioned.

"No. He was found near Moon Lake, his horse nearby. As we put it together, his horse shied at something, maybe a rattler, and threw him. He must have landed the wrong way and snapped his neck," Doc Elton said.

"Maybe his horse didn't shy at anything. Maybe it was no accident," Fargo said. "Maybe Ellie Willis didn't come down with a mysterious coma."

"Those are strong words, Fargo," the doctor said.

"Maybe true ones," Fargo said. "Let's start with this." He handed Doc Elton the note and sat back while he read it and looked up at him when he finished. He recounted the attack by the fake Indians and his meeting with the young woman who claimed to be Ellie Willis, leaving out some of the steamier details. When he finished, Doc Elton's long face seemed longer. "It's plain now that she kept me in Duchess just long enough so Ellie Willis would die before I might get to her."

"I'm without words," Doc Elton said. "And certainly without answers. This is all very disturbing. I know there's ongoing bad blood up at Moon Lake, but I don't see how any of this fits in with that."

"What kind of bad blood?" Fargo questioned.

"Between Joe Barry and the small landowners around Moon Lake," Doc Elton said. "But Ben Adams worked for the Barry ranch as a stable hand.

"And Ellie Willis?"

"She did free-lance sewing work and lived with Ben just outside of town."

"It's plain she knew Ben was afraid of something. That's why she sent me the letter," Fargo said. "It's also damn plain that someone found out she'd sent for me. Somebody tried to have me killed before I got here, by an Indian attack so there wouldn't be a lot of questions. But whoever it is was taking no chances. If the attack failed, which it did, they had this woman waiting for me. It's damn plain she had orders to keep me in Duchess long enough for the real Ellie Willis to die."

"These are terrible things you're saying," the doctor muttered, his face drawn.

"I'm not finished. Could Ellie Willis have been poisoned?" Fargo asked.

Doc Elton stared into space for more than a minute before answering. "I never considered that, but it's possible. There are poisons that affect every part of the body, nervous system, heart, brain. Sudden comalike symptoms would be entirely possible," he said. "My God, what's going on here?"

"I don't know, but the quickest way to find out is to catch up to a lying little piece of baggage," Fargo said and rose to his feet. "Meanwhile, I'd like our little talk to stay strictly between us."

"Absolutely. If the things you've suggested prove true, you can count on my help in any way I can give," the doctor said.

"Good," Fargo said and accepted the handshake as he left. Outside he swung onto the Ovaro and turned the horse back toward Duchess. In the distance Moon Lake grew a deeper blue as the sun's rays slanted from the horizon line. When he reached Duchess the day was beginning to fade, and he drew up to the stage depot. A man seated on a chair with only two back rungs looked up.

"If you come for the stage, you're too late, mister. She left this morning," he said.

"You see all the passengers?" Fargo asked.

"I did."

"Was there a woman, good-looking with blond curls?" Fargo questioned.

"Yes, traveling alone," the man said.

"Where's the stage headed?" Fargo asked.

"Southeast, into Colorado. But the first stop is Crater. Ought to be there soon after dark if there's no Indian trouble. It's an overnight stop. She'll go on come morning."

"Obliged," Fargo said and put the pinto into a trot. He picked up the stage wheel tracks beyond town and followed along a curving road until night descended. He halted under a bur oak and laid out his bedroll, pulled sleep to himself, and woke when the moon was in the midnight sky. He took to the saddle again, grateful the stage had stayed on a marked road through the low hills, the wheel marks plain enough in the moonlight.

He made good time in the cool of the night, but it was still a long ride, one that took the stage more than a day to make so he kept going as the sun rose, and he reached Crater a little before noon. The stage had pulled out three hours earlier, he was told, but he had expected that. In fact he was over an hour earlier than he'd hoped. He took a half hour to feed and water the pinto before he rode again, keeping to a steady trot. The wheel marks moved across wide, flat, dry land, and as low, rocky hill country began to edge the plains, he paused to examine the wheel tracks again. They were less dry, the edges less crumbly. The stage was only a few hours ahead.

He sent the Ovaro onward again, veered off into the low hills, and stayed in them as he kept the horse at a fast trot.

The sun was beginning to slide toward the horizon when he spotted the stage. He spurred the Ovaro on as he stayed in the rock-lined high ground. Keeping out of sight he drew abreast of the wagon and saw it was not a heavy Concord but a Brewster road-coach, a lighter and smaller vehicle. The road-coach couldn't hold as many passengers as the Concord inside but it carried a high seat in the rear for extra riders. Brewsters were used by many short-haul stage lines where most of the terrain was flat, easy-riding land, and it took only four horses to pull them where as the heavy Concords used six. A shotgun rider sat beside the driver, he saw, usual practice for stagecoach travel. Fargo moved the Ovaro on through the hills, riding a few hundred yards ahead of the stage before he swerved from the rocks and rode down to halt as the stage approached.

He held up one hand, and the stage driver reined his team to a stop. Fargo saw the guard quietly shift the shotgun across his lap to him. The Trailsman walked the pinto slowly and halted alongside the stage. "What can we do for you, mister?" the driver queried, and Fargo saw the guard keep the shotgun barrel pointed at him. Inside the road-coach Fargo saw a well-dressed man, a woman, and a four-year-old. His eyes paused at the face with blond curls and the wide, sensuous mouth. She looked at him and then quickly away, her face tight.

Fargo turned his eyes to the driver. "I'll be taking one of your passengers," he said and saw the driver and the guard exchange quick glances.

"You a lawman?" the driver asked.

"No," Fargo admitted.

"Well, now, I don't think we can let you do that, mister," the driver said. "You just can't go taking people off a stagecoach."

"This is an emergency," Fargo said.

Her voice interrupted, and Fargo saw her lean out of the stage window. "Don't listen to him. He's an old boyfriend. He's keeps chasing me. I don't want any part of him," she said.

Bitch, Fargo muttered as he saw the guard raise the shotgun from his lap. "I think you'd best ride on, mister," the driver said sternly.

Fargo sighed. He didn't want the situation to get out of hand, no shooting, nobody getting killed for no reason. It could easily do that, he realized, the driver and guard now protective. "Whatever you say. I don't want trouble." He shrugged and turned the horse in a circle toward the rear of the stage.

The driver snapped the reins, and the stage began to move forward. The shotgun-toting guard turned and when he saw Fargo still standing in place, he faced front.

Fargo hung back another moment, and his hand went to the lariat hanging from its saddle strap. He had the rope spinning in the air as he sent the Ovaro charging forward, the horse going into an instant gallop. The guard heard the hooves and turned in his seat again, his eyes widening in surprise. He tried to bring the shotgun up and around, but he was in an awkward position, and before he had the gun raised the lariat was dropping over his shoulders. Fargo yanked hard, and the guard flew from the seat and hit the ground. The driver reined up and thought better about trying for his gun as he saw the Colt in Fargo's hand. The guard lay on the ground, shaking cobwebs from his head, the lariat still tight around him.

"I don't want anyone to get hurt," Fargo said to the driver. "Toss your gun down, nice and easy." The man obeyed, and his pistol landed on the ground beside the front wheel of the stage. The guard had pushed up on both knees, the shotgun well out of his reach as he glowered up at Fargo, whose eyes bored into the coach. "You getting out or do I have to drag you out?" he growled.

Her lips tightened, she pushed on the door latch and stepped down from the stage. She wore a dark blue jacket and skirt, a white blouse, and in one hand she carried a small, soft leather travel pouch. She walked toward him, glowering at him as she did. He holstered the Colt, took the travel pouch from her, and hung it from the saddle horn. He reached one hand down for her and pulled her up onto the saddle in front of him.

"Take the lariat off," he said to the guard still on his knees. The man rose and pulled the lasso from around him. "Now go your way. Sorry for the interruption," Fargo said as he gathered the lariat in, put the pinto into a fast canter, and rode north across the plateau.

He cast a glance back, just in case, but the guard was clambering onto the stage, and the driver sent the team forward. Fargo turned the horse northwest, climbing through the low rocky hills as the sun touched the horizon.

"Now, you're going to talk, honey," he said.

"I don't have much to talk about, honest," she said.

"What's your real name? Let's start with that," Fargo growled.

"Betty Smith," she said.

"Sounds as fake as you are," he commented.

"It's not. That's my name," she insisted, and Fargo only grunted as he saw the dusk rapidly turning into night. The rock terrain of the hills gave way to mountain ash, hackberry, and shadbush. He chose a pair of hackberry trees with their spreading branches entangled, drew to a halt, and climbed from the saddle. "We'll bed down here," he said and gestured to some lengths of dry wood scattered nearby. "Collect enough for a fire," he added as he unsaddled the Ovaro and laid out his bedroll.

She had the wood stacked into a small pyramid when he finished, and he lighted it to give them a small fire as the black of night enveloped the hills. She sat down beside him as he warmed some beef jerky from his saddlebag. "Tell me the rest," he said. "Who hired you?"

"I don't know," she said.

"Honey, my patience is on a very short rein," Fargo warned.

"Two men hired me. They never used any names," she said.

"They gave you a story to tell. They had to coach you," Fargo said.

"Yes. I was to act as though I were someone by the name of Ellie Willis. They gave me some background about her and Ben Adams. I was to wait at the inn. If you showed up, I was to keep you there for two nights," Betty Smith said.

"Long enough for the real Ellie Willis to die before I reached her," Fargo said bitterly.

The woman stared at him, her mouth dropping open. "I didn't know anything about that. I didn't know about anybody dying. That's the truth," she said, and Fargo's eyes probed at her. She sounded sincerely upset. But then she'd put on a good act as Ellie Willis.

"What else?" he grunted.

"There's nothing else. That's all they told me," she said as he handed her one of the warm strips of jerky, which she hungrily attacked.

"How'd they come to pick you?" he questioned.

"I was waitressing at the saloon in Moonside. I'd been there only a few weeks. I was trying to earn enough money to go my way," she said.

"Where'd you come from?" he pressed.

"Big Sandy in the Wyoming territory. I had a man there until he stranded me. When I took the job at the saloon in Moonside, I made no secret about wanting to go my way. Then these two men came to see me one night. They told me what I'd have to do and offered me five hundred dollars. Jesus, you *know* I said yes," she told him.

"And you didn't ask them anything more?" Fargo said.

"Figured it wasn't any of my business. They came to see me three times to make sure I had my story down right."

"And they never mentioned their names."

"Never, swear to God."

"You'd recognize them if you saw them again, of course," Fargo said.

She thought for a moment. "Sure, I guess so."

"We're going to find out," Fargo said grimly.

"Now wait a minute. What if they're not around anymore? What if they took off?" she protested.

"Then you're in a lot of trouble, honey," Fargo said.

"That's not fair," she said.

"Ellie Willis and Ben Adams are dead. I'm interested in truth, not fairness," he said. "If you're telling the truth, it's likely the men who hired you are still around."

"God, I hope so," she muttered.

He rose to his feet and tossed her the travel pouch. "Get yourself ready to sleep," he said, and she pushed to her feet as the fire burned low, removed her clothes, and stood naked with an air of defiance. She took a nightgown from the pouch and didn't rush to put it on. When she did, he took a length of lariat and tied one end of it around her wrist and the other end around his. "Just in case you've any ideas about running," he said. He lay down atop the bedroll that was wide enough to include her, and she settled in beside him.

"I lied to you. I played the part they paid me to play," she said. "Except in bed. I didn't lie then. I enjoyed it." She paused, rose on one elbow, and the swell of one breast curved over the neck of the nightgown. "I'd like to prove that," she said.

"Maybe, after you prove the rest of your story," he said.

"I suppose I can't blame you," she muttered as she lay back on the bedroll.

"That's right. Now get to sleep. We've a hard day's ride tomorrow," he said and felt the pull on his wrist as she turned on her side. He slept with his other hand over the rope around his wrist. He woke three times during the night as he felt the pull on the rope, but each time it was only her restless turning. When morning came he rose, untied the lariat, and found a small stream for them to wash in.

She again let her body entice him and half pouted when he refused to respond. When she was in the saddle with him, she leaned back against him, the softness of her rear pressing against his crotch. But she didn't utter a word as the day passed and the shadows began to lengthen.

It was only as they neared Moonside that she spoke. "Everything I told you was the truth. They hired me to do a job. I didn't know about anyone dying," she said.

"I'd like to believe you. I hope I can," Fargo said as the night swept down on them. He reached the town a few hours after nightfall, and he heard the apprehension in her voice as she half turned in the saddle to look at him.

"You can't take me to meet everybody in town," she said.

"Why not? It's not a big place," he answered.

"What if they're from out of town?" she asked.

"I thought about that. We'll just go visiting," he said.

"What happens if I see them?" she said.

"You just tell me, nice and quietly," he said.

"And then?"

"You're off the hook."

"You'll owe me stage fare," she sniffed.

"Fair enough," he said as he halted the Ovaro outside the saloon.

"We start here. You say this is where they came to you. There's a good chance they'll stop in again. You can eat and watch at the same time," Fargo said and swung from the saddle.

Inside the saloon he sat with Betty Smith at a small table against the wall, which afforded an unobstructed view of the men standing at the bar. He ordered drinks and the single food item available, beef sandwiches. He watched her eat hungrily as she surveyed the customers who came and went at the bar, some of whom cast nods of recognition at her. At one point the bartender came over, a portly man with a genial manner.

"Didn't expect to see you back here," he said to her.

"Just an unexpected visit," she said. "This is my friend, Fargo."

The man nodded and Fargo offered a smile. "Seen Doc Elton today?" he asked.

"You know Doc?" the bartender said. "No, he's not one of my regulars. But I see him outside sometimes. Good man."

"That he is," Fargo said, and the bartender returned to his bar as four new customers arrived.

Fargo saw one of the newcomers, a thin man with a thin face and a drooping mustache, stare at Betty Smith for a long moment before turning to order his drink. "You know him?" Fargo questioned her.

"I think I've seen him in here before," she said.

"He gave you a hard look," Fargo commented.

"Maybe he was just surprised to see me here as a customer," she said.

"Maybe," Fargo said, his eyes on the man. He kept his eyes on the thin figure as the man downed his drink in one quick draw and turned, cast another frowning glance at Betty, and hurried out of the saloon.

"Stay here," Fargo said as he rose and strode to the door, hurring outside where he halted and heard the sound of hoofbeats galloping into the darkness. The frown was still on his brow when he returned to Betty. "You're sure he wasn't one of the men who hired you?" Fargo asked.

"I'm sure. Wouldn't I tell you. God, that's what I want to do," she returned, and he acknowledged the truth of her answer.

"Well, he was more than surprised to see you. He was very bothered. I'd guess he hightailed it out of here to tell somebody," Fargo said. "He may be back with help. If he shows, you hit the floor and stay under the table." Betty nodded. Fargo ordered drinks and sat back against the wall, his hand resting on the butt of the Colt at his hip. But the thin-faced man didn't return, and the hours ticked away until he and the woman were the only customers left in the saloon.

"I'm closing up," the bartender said, and Fargo nodded as he rose to his feet.

"Good night," Fargo said, holding Betty by the

elbow as he walked from the saloon. Outside he halted, his eyes sweeping the dark and silent single street. "It's too late to pay Doc Elton a call. We'll bed out tonight." He climbed onto the Ovaro and Betty pulled herself up to sit in front of him. He moved the horse at a walk through the still street, his eyes searching the shadows by the buildings on both sides, the Colt held in his hand. He strained his ears, listening for sounds, any sounds other than Betty's steady breathing. He was approaching the last two buildings of the town when he heard it, the soft, slapping sound of a cheek band when a horse tosses its head.

"Jump," he yelled and pulled her with him as he leaped from the saddle. The first shots came instantly as Fargo hit the ground with Betty, and then the riders raced from behind the buildings. He glimpsed four of them firing in volleys as they charged forward. "Roll," he cried as he heard the bullets thud into the ground. He drew his own Colt and flung himself into the blackest shadows against the building. The riders were racing back and forth, laying down a barrage, and Fargo heard the shots slam into the wood inches from his head. Lying prone, he fired and saw one of the riders topple from the saddle. He stayed flattened and drew a bead on another dark form racing past, fired, and saw the man go down. The remaining two attackers swerved and galloped off into the darkness. Fargo knew his last shot missed.

He rose and ran to where Betty Smith lay facedown on the ground. "They're gone," he said, but she didn't move, and he felt his stomach tighten as he dropped to one knee beside her. "Aw, Christ," he groaned as he saw the four widening circles of red. Gently he turned her over and swore under his breath. Betty Smith would not prove anything again, not ever. The gunmen had made certain of that and, rage sweeping through him, he rose and stepped to the nearest of the two he had brought down. He peered down at the man, an ordinary face twisted in deathly pain. He strode to the second one, turned the body over with a kick of his boot, and saw the thin-faced man who had fled from the saloon

He had run to tell someone who'd sent the attackers back with orders to be sure and kill Betty Smith. The four fatal bullets proved that they'd fired the majority of their volleys at her, and he damned their souls for it as he saw other figures hurrying toward him on foot The first to reach him was a tall man with a black duster wrapped around him, his face lined and severe.

"What happened here?" the man asked.

"The lady and I were drygulched," Fargo said. "Who are you?"

"Ed Brumby," the man said.

"The town undertaker," Fargo said. "Doc Elton mentioned your name."

"You know Doc?" the undertaker asked, and Fargo nodded. The man turned to one of three other figures that had appeared. "Go fetch Doc Elton," he said, and Fargo gestured to Betty Smith as the other man hurried away.

"I want a proper burial for her," he said. "I'll pay the cost."

Brumby nodded as he waited, and only a few minutes passed when the man returned with Doc Elton, his spare figure in a frayed bathrobe.

"You know this feller, Doc?" the undertaker asked.

"Yes, I do," the doctor said. "If he says he was drygulched, that's what happened." He stepped closer to the two slain attackers and peered at them.

"Know them?" Fargo queried.

"They worked for Joe Barry," Doc Elton said.

"Good enough," Fargo grunted. "That gives me a place to start."

"Ed will take care of everything here. He'll send a man to the Barry place. Come back to my place with me," Doc Elton said, and Fargo gathered the Ovaro and followed the tall, spare figure to the house. "I need a cup of coffee," the doctor said as he went inside.

Fargo lowered himself onto a high stool beside a kitchen table. "Sorry I had to get you up at this hour. You still want to help me? This is getting nastier."

"You still want to pursue this?" Doc Elton asked as he served the coffee in tin mugs.

"Damn right. For Ben Adams first, then for Ellie, and now for Betty Smith. She was just hired help, I'm convinced. And last but not least, for myself. I don't take to being drygulched and damn near murdered."

"I'll help, in any way I can, but that might not be much," Doc said.

"It looks more and more as if this Joe Barry is behind everything. I'd say he was afraid that Ben Adams had found out something, and he made sure Ben wouldn't tell anyone," Fargo ventured.

"You'll need a lot more than suspicions against Joe Barry. He's a powerful, smart man, and he has two mean sons to do his dirty work. Don't underestimate him."

"I won't. But I'll be paying him a visit. What's this bad blood you spoke about between Barry and the small landholders?" Fargo asked.

"Something about Barry pressuring them for their lands. They've formed a loose association. I'll introduce you, if you like."

"Good. Maybe their problems with Joe Barry have nothing to do with this, and then maybe they do. I know you don't see a connection, and I don't either, so far. But I aim to dig deeper."

"First, how about some sleep, not that there's much left of the night. You can use one of the rooms in my sanatorium," Doc Elton said.

"I'll take you up on that," Fargo said and finished the coffee. He rose, weariness dropping over him suddenly. Nothing had gone right so far. Whoever was behind the slaughter was having everything *his* way. It was time to change that.

3

Fargo slept well, and Doc Elton had coffee on when he went into the kitchen. "I want to visit Ben Adams's place. I take it Ellie Willis still lived there until she fell into that coma a week ago," Fargo said.

"That's right. I brought her here to my place then. She was in no condition to leave alone," Doc Elton said. "It's a small house, half mile south of Moon Lake beside a twisted peachleaf willow. You can't miss it or the tree."

"After that I'll be paying a visit to Joseph Barry," Fargo said.

"All you'll get there is smooth answers," Doc said.

"I just want him to know the game has changed; there's a new player on hand. If he's behind this, he'll get the message."

"Take care," the doctor said as Fargo finished the coffee and went outside.

He saddled the Ovaro and set out at once for Moon Lake, which turned out to be larger than it had appeared from a distance. Houses, farms, and cattle pens dotted the land set back from the shoreline, he noted as he paused on a high rise. He'd go down for a closer look another time, as he rode south, following the directions Doc Elton had given him. He found the twisted willow and the small frame house not far from it. Dismounting, he pushed the door open and halted, his eyes taking in the total disarray inside. Dressers lay overturned, their draws spilled out, mattresses ripped open, clothes strewn across both rooms. Fargo picked his way through the result of what had obviously been a search for something.

But what, he wondered as he turned and walked outside, closing the door behind him. He added two more questions. Had the searchers found what they were after? Or hadn't they? He climbed onto the pinto and turned the horse toward Joseph Barry's place. Perhaps he could kill two birds with one stone—find out the answer to his questions and the two new ones he'd just come upon. He returned to Moon Lake and circled it, as Doc Elton had directed, getting a closer view of some of the homesteads bordering the lake. Most seemed neat and modest enough, and he rode on, moving farther from the lake until he came to the large stone and log ranch house.

Three bunkhouses spread out to the right of it, barns and corrals beyond. A fair-sized herd of white-faced steers spread through the corrals, and Fargo moved the pinto slowly along a road that curved its way to the main house. Two men standing unobtrusively at each side of the house watched him halt and dismount. A man emerged from inside the house before he had a chance to knock—large, powerfully built with salt-and-pepper hair. He wore a dark green checked shirt and carried a Remington-Rider at his side, a five-shot double-action gun with a brass trigger guard. Fargo's eyes moved across a strong face where a confident imperiousness almost masked the hard arrogance in it.

Two younger men came up behind the man, one smallish with close-cropped brown hair, belligerence in his stance. The other one was taller with the older man's strong face but with more meanness in the mouth.

"Joseph Barry?" Fargo asked.

"That's me," the man said. "These are my boys, Jed and Seth. And who may you be?"

Fargo smiled and wondered if the question was just a moment of cleverness. "Name's Fargo . . . Skye Fargo," he said.

"What brings you visiting, Fargo?" Joseph Barry asked.

"Last night I was drygulched in town, and a young woman I was with was killed. Murdered might be a better word. They made sure they got her," Fargo said. "I found out that two of them worked for you."

"You accusing me of having something to do with it?" the man shot back.

"Not yet," Fargo said. "I'm asking for answers."

"You watch your tongue, mister," the smaller one snapped, his hot temper instant in his eyes.

"They worked here," Fargo said, ignoring the youth, his eyes ice blue as they held on Joseph Barry. "You tell me the rest."

He saw the senior Barry back down, the arrogance leaving his tone. "I'm sorry for what happened to your lady friend. I know about the incident. One of Ed Brumby's men stopped by. Yes, those two men worked for me, but I employ a lot of men. All I ask is they give me a good day's work. I don't know anything about the rest of their lives, and I don't make a point of asking. I wouldn't have any idea why they'd drygulch you and kill the woman."

Fargo's glance shifted to take in the land and corrals beyond the house, and he saw a good number of ranch hands at work or lounging by the barns. "It seems you keep on a lot of hands," he said. "More than most spreads this size."

"I have my own way of using hands. I send a lot of them out with the cattle to range graze. Truth is, I've a lot of turnover, and I'm always looking for new hands," Barry said. "As for the two who took part in drygulching you and the lady, I'd guess there was something more than you know behind it. Sorry I can't help you more than that."

"I'm sorry, too. You see, I came here to help an old friend of mine who it seems was in some kind of trouble. He worked for you, too, I hear. Ben Adams."

"Old Ben Adams. Sure, worked here for a good long time. Terrible about his being killed in a dumb accident," the man said.

"Maybe it wasn't an accident. Maybe it had something to do with the varmints who attacked me last night. I aim to find out," Fargo said.

"You accusing again, mister? I warned you," the smaller son snapped and stepped forward angrily, one hand on the butt of his six-gun.

"Simmer down, sonny, or I'll have to step on you," Fargo said softly.

The youth's mouth dropped open, and he was about to explode when Joseph Barry's voice cut in. "Now, Jed, you calm down. The man's had a personal loss. He's got a right to ask questions," the man said soothingly. "I'm sorry we just can't answer them. But if I hear anything, I'll be glad to let you know. Where can I reach you?"

"Doc Elton will know," Fargo said. "I'm going back to his place now. Tonight I'll be going to Ben Adams's place. I knew Ben for a long time. If he's left anything for me, I'll know where to find it. I know where he likes to hide things. Maybe then I'll get some answers."

"Good idea," Joseph Barry said, his face bland. He'd be a good man in a poker game, Fargo decided as he climbed onto the Ovaro and set off. Perhaps Barry had told him the truth. Perhaps Barry hired men without questions and neither knew nor cared what outside things they did. Maybe. Fargo didn't take to that explanation. Barry had far too many ranch hands for the size of his spread. That didn't fit, either. But he had planted the bait. He'd see if anyone took it. He rode back to Doc Elton's and had to wait two hours while the doctor finished treating a gunshot wound that required an operation.

Finally he sat in Doc Elton's small office and told him what he'd done and what he'd found at Ben's place. "Seems to me you're setting yourself up to get shot," Doc said.

"I don't expect that to happen. I'll be ready if somebody comes calling at Ben's place," Fargo said. "Ben had learned something, that's damn clear now. Somebody killed him to keep him quiet and then took care of Ellie Willis in case he'd told her what he'd learned. No matter what Barry claims, two of the men who drygulched me worked for him. I'd say it sure points in his direction."

"Yes, but all you have is suspicions," Doc reminded him.

"For now. Maybe that'll change soon," Fargo said.

"Have a beef sandwich before you go," Doc Elton said. "You could have a long night's wait."

Fargo agreed and enjoyed the sandwich and a cup of good coffee before he took to the saddle as the day began to drift into night. He reached the small house soon after dark, tethered the Ovaro in a thick cluster of shadbush, and approached the house on foot. He paused as he neared it, scanning the land around it as he listened. He neither saw nor heard anything, and he carefully pushed the door open, the Colt in his hand. Only silence greeted him. He stepped inside, closing the door after him, stumbled over a box, and sank down on the torn mattress in the middle of the floor. He sat in the pitch blackness with the Colt in his lap; the inky dark lightened a fraction as the moon rose and cast a pale glow against the window.

He had waited not more than an hour when he picked up the soft sounds of hoofbeats moving slowly outside, halting, and then silence. The scrape of boots on the ground reached him—in front of the house, more along both sides. Fargo lifted the Colt and pointed it at the still closed doorway. He scowled as he heard more footsteps. They seemed to be circling the house—probably to make certain no one was hiding at the rear. Suddenly he heard a hard thud against the front door as though a log had been pushed against it.

The scowl deepened as he rose to one knee, the Colt still aimed at the door. He heard a strange sound as if water were being thrown against the house. He drew in deeply, and his nostrils quivered—not water, but the sharp odor of kerosene.

"Shit," he swore aloud as he rose and half ran, stumbling, falling against the litter and finally reaching the door. He slammed his shoulder against it, but it didn't give. A log had been wedged against it. Then the darkness gave way to an orange light, and he heard the crackle of flames. He drew back from the door, cursing under his breath as he saw the flames rising on all four sides of the house.

The old wood burned quickly, and the sharp odor of smoke rolled into the room through the cracks in the wallboards. It seemed only seconds for the room to fill with smoke, and he flung himself on the floor. The flames were high now, almost up to the roof as the fire consumed the old house. They had done a good job dousing the place, Fargo thought bitterly as he lay on the floor. Most of the smoke still rose upward, leaving him a few inches of breathing space. But the smoke would grow denser and roll downward to fill up the last bit of air along the floor. And even if it didn't, the roof would soon come crashing down on him.

The smoke diffused the flame so a soft orange glow permeated the room. Fargo spied a sheet on the floor a few feet away, crawled to it and, holding his breath, he rose and whipped the sheet around himself, covering every part of his body and leaving only a slit to see through. He ran wrapped in the sheet and reached the window just as the glass shattered from the heat and showered him with burning bits of fire. Calling on all the strength in his leg muscles, he leaped headfirst through the window and the wall of flames engulfing the house.

He hit the ground, aware the sheet around him was on fire. He rolled furiously, shedding the sheet as he did and leaped to his feet, kicking away the last of the burning fabric. He swept the scene with quick, angry eyes, the house now entirely consumed by flames. But the fire-setters had left and, straining his ears over the crackle of the flames, Fargo heard the sound of hoofbeats receding in the night. He spun, raced to the Ovaro, and leaped onto the saddle. The horse was in full gallop in seconds. The attackers had been so confident, they had just done their work and left, certain that if he were inside he'd not get out alive and that if he hadn't arrived yet he'd find only ashes when he did.

Fargo spurred the Ovaro through a stand of hackberry, letting the carpet of leaves help deaden the sound of the Ovaro, and when he emerged he saw the five horsemen moving casually down a hill under the moonlight. He saw them start to turn and glance back as he charged down at them, but he had the Colt in his hand.

"Surprise, you bastards," he shouted as he fired. Two of the men toppled from their horses, and the other three scattered, spurring their mounts on. He swung after the nearest one, fired again, and the man flew sideways from the saddle. Fargo drew to a halt beside him and saw the man's body lay lifeless. He turned back to the other two. One showed a stream of red from his temple, and the other lay in a pool of his own blood.

Neither would tell any tales, Fargo grunted as he rode on. But the two who got away would be reporting back to Joseph Barry, that was now clear. The bait had been tossed only to him and he'd taken it. It was really stretching the long arm of coincidence to think that someone else just happened along at that moment, and when Fargo returned to Doc Elton, the doctor agreed completely.

"You're lucky you got out," Doc Elton said.

"Not even singed," Fargo said, and the doctor shook his head in awe. "And now we know but we can't prove. We know Joseph Barry's in back of it, all of it, Ben Adams's accident, Ellie Willis's dying, and the attempts on my life. I'm not forgetting about poor Betty Smith, but she was just a bit player."

"We've no proof against Barry, as you said. But if we knew why, we might have that proof. There's got to be a damn good reason behind it," the doctor said.

"Whatever it is that Ben found out," Fargo said. "I can't see any connection between this and whatever bad blood there is between Barry and the folks around the lake, but I'm not ruling out anything. I'd like to meet with them, ask questions. Maybe I'll come onto something."

"It's worth a try," Doc said. "I'll ride up to Orville Dent's place tonight and have him set up a meeting with everyone for the morning."

"Much obliged," Fargo said.

"Meanwhile I think you could do with a drink. There's whiskey in the cabinet," Doc said.

"Good. Best prescription you ever gave out, Doc."

Doc Elton nodded as he walked out. Fargo found the whiskey and relaxed with a glass of the bracing liquid. He was dozing in the chair when Doc Elton finally returned.

"All set for the morning. I've Edith Atkind due in tomorrow so I can't go with you. Go to Orville Dent's place. Direct north. He raises hogs. You won't miss it," Doc said. "Keep me posted."

"I will," Fargo said. "Now I'll take advantage of

that room again for the night." He left quickly, shed clothes, and fell into the cot, aware that he had narrowly missed becoming a cinder.

He slept heavily and woke with the morning sun, had coffee with Doc Elton, and rode northward to Moon Lake. He found Orville Dent's place just by following his nose to the unmistakable odor of hogs. He counted ten horses tethered outside a modest house as he dismounted near a half dozen pigpens filled with good Polands in back of the house. Orville Dent greeted him, a pudgy, round-faced man who faintly resembled his hogs. The others were lined up around the room.

"My wife, Sarah," Dent introduced, and Fargo nodded to an equally round-faced woman. "John Otis," Dent said, gesturing to the first figure against the wall. "Ted and Amy Olson. They have chickens. Abe Abelson and Mary. Abe's retired but he's very much a part of our community. Sam Foreman and Kay, quarter horses, Lem and Carrie Carter, cattle, along with John Otis, Alton Harris and Imogen. Alton's a trapper and he wants to open a trading store by the lake. Last, certainly not least, Madge Downey. Madge has a good business selling the fine quilts she weaves."

Fargo took in a young woman, dark blond with brown eyes, a wide face, attractive and open, combining a thin, sensitive air with full, very sensual lips. Tall and slender, she wore a tan shirt that was nicely filled with the long line of more than modest breasts. She saw his eyes go to a somewhat brooding, intense dark-haired young man standing next to her.

"This is Terence Noonan," she said. "Terence has been working for me for the past two weeks."

Fargo nodded back at the young man.

"I've filled in everyone with what Doc Elton told me, Fargo," Orville Dent said. "It's terrible, real terrible. Joe Barry and his stinking sons are bad news. But we can't figure any connection between this and our troubles with him."

"Tell me more about your troubles," Fargo said.

John Otis spoke up, rubbing one hand along his black beard. "Barry wants to buy us out, and we've all refused, it's as simple as that. We can't figure why he wants our lands. God knows he's got enough himself, and he has water rights to let his steers drink at the lake. But he keeps harassing us, threatening us, getting folks nervous as all hell."

"He got old Ed Craaley off his land. Ed's wife met with a sudden drowning accident, and Ed sold his land to Barry and left," Ted Olson volunteered. "But Ed's land is at the far north end of the lake so it's not part of our properties."

"We've a proposition for you, Fargo," Orville Dent cut in. "We're all scared, real scared. Barry's hiring a lot of men. We're afraid of what he might be planning. We need to be organized. We need someone who'll fight back for us, someone able to deal with men like Joe Barry. From what we hear, you're just the man for us. We'll pay you to find out what he's planning and stop him."

"First, I couldn't do it alone. Anything I do would need your working with me," Fargo said.

"You just tell us what to do," Abe Abelson said. "Seems to us we've got a common enemy. You want to know if he killed Ben Adams and why, and we want him off our backs."

"Both things may be connected. I can't say they are, not yet, but they could be. Maybe Ben found out what he was planning to do to you folks, and that's why he was killed."

"All the more reason for you to help us," Alton Harris said, the others' faces a sober ring facing him.

"All right, you've got a deal," Fargo said. "For Ben and Ellie and for all of you."

"That's real good news," Orville Dent said.

"First thing I want is to get somebody inside Joe Barry's operation. It has to be somebody we can trust but that he'll accept," Fargo said.

"I could do it," the young man beside Madge Downey said. "I've been working for Madge for only two weeks. I'm the newest one here. I'll tell him I didn't like her pay, and I heard about the real good money he was offering. He'll take me."

"I believe he will. He'd enjoy hiring away one of your people," Fargo said.

"No."

The flat word hung in the air, and he turned to where Madge Downey stood with her lips tightened. "I don't like it. It'll be too dangerous for Terence, for anybody. I don't like the whole idea," she said.

"It's the only way. I need an inside contact," Fargo said.

"Then get someone on your own," she said crossly.

"It'd be best if it was someone I can trust completely, one of your people," Fargo said not ungently, but her eyes stayed darkly angry.

"I'm against it," Madge Downey snapped.

"We've an agreement here," Orville Dent interjected. "We put things to a vote. All those who feel Madge is right, raise your right hand. All those who go along with Fargo's plan, raise your left hand." Fargo watched the hands go up, and Madge's was the only right hand. He saw her lips tighten as she shrugged.

"Looks as though I've been outvoted," she murmured, refusing to meet his eyes.

"You go on home," Fargo said to Terence. "I'll stop by later, and we'll plan detailed moves, just the two of us. Now, for the rest of you, I want you to start lining up as many good men as you can trust. I'm sure you've all got relatives, cousins, uncles, people you can call in when the time comes."

"What are you thinking, Fargo?" Orville Dent asked.

"Barry has a lot of men and he's hiring more. We may need to match his strength. I'm not sure, but it's time to prepare," Fargo said.

"Glad you're leading us, Fargo," John Otis said as he filed out with the others. Madge Downey was last to leave the room, and Fargo stepped beside her.

"I'm sorry you don't share John Otis's feelings," he ventured.

"What I feel doesn't matter. I was outvoted," she said.

"It matters to me," Fargo said.

She halted and her brown eyes searched his face. "Just being gracious?" she asked.

"No, I'd like everybody's cooperation. More important, I'd like you to believe in me," he said.

"Is that important?" Madge Downey asked.

"Yes, but not so important I'm going to back down on anything," he said.

She smiled and suddenly was terribly lovely, her wide face instantly warm. "That's being honest. I appreciate honesty, even when I don't like it. You don't find it often," she said. He watched her walk outside, her tall slenderness graceful, hips swaying but her rear flat and tight. She swung onto a tan quarter horse with an easy movement and rode away, Terence Noonan alongside her on a gray gelding. Fargo swung onto the Ovaro and rode in the opposite direction, taking a slow circle around the entire lake, and when he finished Moon Lake was an enigma. It was a pretty lake, prettier than many, but otherwise seemed completely ordinary. Perhaps Joseph Barry simply wanted more land for himself, he speculated. But he rejected the thought. There was plenty of land for the taking just behind Barry's ranch. Plainly he didn't want anything but the land bordering the lake.

There had to be a special reason. Fargo frowned as he halted at the shoreline and dismounted. He knelt down and dug his hands into the soft soil of the lakeside. He felt nothing different. He walked along the bank, the horse following, and paused from time to time to examine the shoreline soil. Finally he climbed back onto the Ovaro and rode from the shoreline, skirted John Otis's place, and moved inland until he reached the modest house where he spotted the gray gelding outside. He also saw neat rows of vegetables growing behind the house, long lines of lettuce, cucumber, squash, tomato, kale and, in the distance, new corn.

Madge Downey came from the house, and he saw she had changed to denim overalls that accentuated her tall slenderness. A white, cotton shirt revealed tiny dark circles at the tip of each breast. "Seems you do more than make quilts," Fargo said with a nod at the farm patch.

"Yes, quilts aren't enough. The produce helps pay the bills. That's why I've a helper, Terence at the moment," she said, and he followed her into a neatly furnished house with yellow curtains on the windows of an airy living room. A thick, woven rug of myriad colors graced the floor, and he glimpsed a weaver's loom in an adjoining room. Terence Noonan came from the rear of the house. "I'll leave you two to make your plans," Madge said and disappeared into the back rooms.

"I'm expecting Barry will take you on. Take a couple of days to work your way in and get the feel of the land. At midnight, four days from now, I'll be at the north end of the lake beside a pair of rocky mountain maples that stand off by themselves."

"I know the place," Terence said.

"Don't worry if you can't get away. I'll be there every midnight. You come when you can," Fargo said.

"I'll find a way," Terence said with his brooding intensity, and Fargo realized he hadn't seen Terence Noonan give a hint of a smile. Plainly a very serious young man, Fargo noted.

"Don't rush it. I'd rather wait than have you make a mistake," Fargo said.

"No mistakes," Terence said and rose to leave with a nod. Madge returned a few moments later.

"He always that serious?" Fargo asked.

"Yes. I'd say he's had a troubled past. But he's trying real hard to turn over a new leaf."

"You like him," Fargo ventured.

"He's been a good worker in the short time he's been here and, as you saw, he has real spirit," Madge said.

"Let's hope it all turns out right," Fargo said.

"I don't like empty hopes. I've had enough of them," she said, and he heard the bitterness in her voice.

"Bad breaks or bad lovers?"

"Both," Madge said. "I bought this land, and I had a man I was engaged to who was going to work it with me. What he did was to leave me and take whatever money I had left over with him."

"Sorry," Fargo said. "No one's come along since then, I take it."

"No one," she said curtly.

"Or is it that you won't let anyone close again?" Fargo said.

She turned her brown eyes on him and studied his face for a long moment. "You're real smart or you're real lucky at guessing," she said.

"Maybe both."

"There have been a few I thought about, but that's all I did," she said thoughtfully.

"Can't keep that up forever, not a woman who looks like you," Fargo said. That'd be like keeping a sunflower out of the sun. It'll just shrivel up in time."

Her smile was thoughtful. "I'll try and remember that," she said as she walked from the house with him. Outside the dark had descended, and Fargo swung onto the pinto as Madge leaned against the door. He took in the contained loveliness of her. Terence Noonan came from the rear of the house to halt before the Ovaro.

"Check with Madge tomorrow. If I've given her my notice you'll know what that means," Terence said.

"I will, and I'll be at the two maples in four

nights. You make it only if you can do it safely," Fargo said.

"I'll find a way," the young man said and moved closer to Madge as Fargo rode away. Fargo returned to Doc Elton's place wondering about a very contained young woman and her young hired hand. Somehow he felt it was more than the ordinary relationship between an employer and her help. At Doc's place he filled the physician in on all that had been decided.

"I'm glad. It's a start, more than they've been able to put together on their own so far," Doc Elton said, and Fargo again took advantage of his offer to stay the night. There'd not be many more chances, he felt certain, and he went to sleep still wondering about Madge Downey and Terence Noonan.

The morning sun woke him, and after he washed and dressed and had coffee with Doc Elton, he rode out toward the lake and saw Joseph Barry, his two sons, and three of their hands moving along a ridge. He followed discreetly and watched them circle Moon Lake, pausing from time to time, but Joseph Barry did nothing that remotely resembled a clue to his thoughts.

Finally they rode on, and Fargo made his way to Madge's place. She greeted him at the door wearing overalls and a short-sleeve cotton shirt that hugged tight against the long curve of her breasts.

"Terence was by. He quit on me," she said with a half smile.

"Sorry about that," Fargo said.

"Hell you are," Madge said, her smile widening. "Truth is I did need him this week. I've squash and pumpkin to bring in, a lot of it."

"I know where you can hire a temporary hand," Fargo said. "For a few days anyway."

"If you mean what I think you do, you're hired," she said. "Put your horse in the barn." He walked the Ovaro to her barn and returned to where she waited for him with a wooden cart. "The squash first, then the pumpkins if we've any daylight left," she said. "Bring as many as you can back here in the cart, then go back with it for another load."

"Yes, ma'am," he said, and she gave a wry smile.

"Sorry, I didn't mean to sound so bossy," she said. "Put 'please' in front of everything I said."

"Good enough." Fargo nodded and went into the farmed and planted land, pulling the cart behind him. He had made at least eight trips and there were still pumpkin to pick up when the dusk came, and Madge called to him from the doorway, a wooden soup ladle in her hand.

"Supper's ready. Come in and wash up," she called, and he hurried into the house remembering why he'd never wanted to be a farmer. When he sat down opposite her across a small wooden table, she had changed the overalls for a skirt and the cotton shirt for a blue blouse. "Transformation," she said. "From boss to hostess."

"I'll take either," Fargo said

"Thanks for all the help," Madge said almost gravely. "Tomorrow morning ought to finish the pumpkin. There'll be time to bring in some lettuce and kale by noon."

"Yes, sir," Fargo said blandly.

"There I go again. I'm sorry.' Her hand reached out, an impulsive gesture, covered his for a moment, and then drew back. "I'm grateful for everything you're doing," she said. "Will you spend the night? There's an empty room in the rear."

"Why not? I can get started early that way," he said and enjoyed the simple but tasty meal she had prepared. She brought out a bottle of brandy when it was over and led him to the living room for an after-dinner drink. She tucked herself onto a settee, her long frame graceful as she leaned back, and he saw the tips of her breasts push tiny points into the blouse.

"I thought about what you said, about withering away. I don't want to do that," she said. "But giving in to your own hungers is just another way of withering away. I'm afraid to do that. That's too easy."

"Yes, I can understand that," he said and felt a surge of sympathy for Madge Downey. All those woman like her, too. Hunger and pride, and the flesh and the spirit, those things could tear at each other, refusing accommodation. "I can't give you an answer, except maybe one," he said.

"What's that?" she inquired.

"Pick and choose," Fargo told her. "On your terms. If it goes well, you're ahead. If it doesn't, it's your call."

She smiled as she rose and cleared away dishes. "I'll have to think about that. You make it sound simple when nothing is simple," she said.

"Some things are, if you don't complicate them," he said, and she gave a shrug of half agreement.

Madge showed him his room, simple and unadorned except for a dresser and big water pitcher and cot.

"See you in the morning," she said and hurried away. He watched her go, tall slenderness, a flat rear that hardly moved as she walked. That contained air was both an outer and inner defense, he decided, and he shed clothes and lay down on the cot. It was more comfortable than it appeared.

He slept quickly and soundly and woke when the new sun came through the lone window of the room. He used the big pitcher to wash and found towels in the dresser. When he went outside, he saw Madge had nearly filled a fruit-rack wagon with movable racks. She wore the cotton white shirt and overalls again and looked girlishly young. "Soon as you bring in some lettuce and kale I'll be driving into town," she said. "I do a good business from the wagon. People wait for me to come, and the rest I sell to the saloon."

He hurried to the neat rows of vegetables with the small cart and soon had brought back enough kale and lettuce to finish filling the fruit-rack wagon. Madge had hitched up the horse, and Fargo saddled the Ovaro and caught up to her as she headed to Moonside.

"I'll pay a visit to Doc Elton while you're selling off your things," he told her, and when they reached town, he waited to watch her set up shop a hundred yards from the saloon. She had customers almost immediately, he noted as he turned away and visited Doc Elton's office.

"Barry hired four more men," Doc said. "He's got to be preparing for something. I hope we're not too late to stop him."

"Keep the faith," Fargo said and accepted Doc's offer of coffee. When he finished, he made his way back into town and saw the small crowd gathered as he neared Madge's wagon. But they were onlookers, not customers, he quickly realized as he heard Madge's voice.

"No, stop that, you bastards," she was shouting, and Fargo pushed the Ovaro through the crowd to see her rushing from one end of the wagon to the other as two men tossed her produce out of the wagon. When she reached one, he stepped back and the other one gleefully flung squash and lettuce into the street.

"Rotten bastards," she bit out as she ran back to the other end of the wagon, and the first man again pulled vegetables into the street. Both men were short, one bald, the other with unkempt brown hair, Fargo saw as he swung to the ground. He started for the nearest of the two men who was laughing as he tossed squash out of the wagon. His unkempt hair flew as he stomped the vegetables into the ground. Words would be a waste of time, Fargo realized. He knew the type: small-minded bullies who understood only one thing.

The man looked up in time to see Fargo's blow smash into his stomach. With a grunt of pain he doubled over and sank to the ground on his knees. Fargo brought a chopping blow down across the back of his head, and the man collapsed facedown amid the smashed squash. Fargo turned, saw the second man fling Madge aside as he saw what had happened, and reach for his gun. He had it out of the holster when Fargo's shot slammed into the gun, and the man yelped in pain as the weapon flew from his hand. "Sonofabitch," he snarled and charged at the big man, his bald head glistening in the sun.

Fargo waited, parried the first two wild swings, and brought up a short, crisp left hook that landed on the man's jaw. The bald-headed figure halted, took a step backward, and Fargo's right crossed and smashed into his abdomen. As he started to double over, Fargo's left caught him on the point of the chin again, lifted him from the ground, and deposited him against the base of a water trough. Fargo stepped to the man, closed one hand around his shirtfront, and yanked him to his feet, tossing him into the water trough. The bald head disappeared under the surface and reappeared sputtering and shocked back into consciousness.

Fargo reached into the trough, pulled the man out, and threw him on the ground. "Goddamn," the man spit out as he pushed to his feet, eying his opponent, as he shook water from himself. Fargo's sweeping right smashed into the man's jaw, and the bald head went backward lancing six feet away on the ground, unconscious again. Fargo turned and saw the other one just starting to push himself from the ground to stand still, arms hanging limply as he shook his head. Fargo took two strides forward, sank another short right into the man's midsection, and the figure collapsed again with a wheezing grunt and lay still.

Fargo turned to Madge and saw less than a half wagon of salable produce left. "What happened?" he asked.

"I'd just set up when they came by and started throwing everything out of the wagon," Madge said.

"You know them?" Fargo asked.

"No, but they seemed to know me. They said, 'Look who's here,' " Madge told him.

Fargo glanced at the onlookers and saw the bartender from the saloon. "You know them?" he questioned.

"They're part of Joe Barry's crew," the bartender answered.

"Those are their horses," Madge said, gesturing to two mounts nearby. "They were leading them when they saw me."

"Joe Barry's crew," Fargo echoed tightly as he stepped to the still unconscious bald-headed one, picked him up as though he were a sack of wheat, and threw him across the horse so he hung face-down. He did the same with the other man and then swung onto the Ovaro. "I'll stop by later," he said to Madge as he gathered the reins of the two other horses in one hand and began to lead the animals and their swaying cargo away.

4

Fargo rode slowly up to Joseph Barry's ranch house. The two figures draped over their horses behind him had regained consciousness along the way, but he had stopped, smashed both in the face, and returned them to limp silence again. Now they were groaning as Fargo halted. Joseph Barry and his two sons emerged from the house. Fargo backed the Ovaro to the two other horses and used his foot to push first the bald-headed one and then the other man from their saddles. Both landed on the ground with dull thuds, and Fargo saw the bald one lift his head to peer up at Joseph Barry through his swollen and bloodied face.

"I understand this garbage belongs to you," Fargo said to Barry. He saw the man's jaw muscles throb as he looked down at the two men, anger barely contained in his face.

"They work for me," Barry said quietly. "What happened?"

"They were destroying Madge Downey's wagon load of produce. I didn't think that was a nice thing to do," Fargo said blandly.

Joseph Barry continued to stare down at the two men, his mouth a thin line. The bald one pushed himself to his knees and gazed up at his boss. "We just thought—" he began.

"Shut up," Barry snapped. "You were stupid fools and you paid for it." He gestured to his sons. "Get these idiots to the bunkhouse. I'll deal with them later." He turned to Fargo as Seth and Jed Barry took the two men away. "I must apologize for the actions of those two, but I can't control everything my men do when they're on their own," he said.

"Yes, you said that once before." Fargo nodded.

"They'll be appropriately disciplined. Please give my regrets to Miss Downey."

"I'll be sure and do that," Fargo said.

"You seem to have a streak of the good samaritan to you, Fargo," Barry said. "That's very commendable, but perhaps you should be more selective about those you rush to help."

"Spell that out some more," Fargo said.

"Many of these small land-holders around the lake are really problems, a rather grubby lot that we could well do without. I'd hate to see you become involved with that kind. Unfortunately Miss Downey is one of them," Barry said.

Fargo smiled inwardly. The man was smooth, his warning couched in cleverly veiled language. "Thanks," Fargo said blandly. "And I'd suggest you keep a tighter rein on what your boys do when they're on their own." He offered a polite nod and rode from the ranch, passing the two Barry boys who exchanged hard glances with him. Jed, the smallish, hot-tempered one, was a youth waiting to explode. The senior Barry was plainly a man who disliked anything outside his control, but Fargo wondered how much control he could exercise over

Jed. Three more men passed Fargo on their way to the Barry place as he took the road north, and he wondered if they were new arrivals. Dusk descended and night was full on the land when he reached Madge's place.

She greeted him at the door, her arms sliding around his neck. "I'd have lost all of it if you hadn't come by," she said, just as quickly drawing her arms back. "I'm really grateful. I sold what was left to the saloon."

"Those two were acting on their own, I'm convinced of that. They thought they'd do their boss a favor," Fargo said.

"They would have, except for you," Madge said. "Sit down, I've dinner ready." He followed her into the house and enjoyed a good meal of boiled chicken and squash with honey. "You'll stay the night?" she asked when the meal ended.

"A good bed's always welcome," Fargo said, and he helped her clear away the dishes and went outside and unsaddled the pinto while she finished.

"You'll be waiting for Terence tomorrow night," Madge said, and he nodded. "Good night, then," she added, and he went into the small room and the cot. He shed his clothes in the dark and stretched out, the sheet lying casually across his groin when he heard the footsteps outside the door.

"May I come in?" Madge's voice asked.

"Why not?" Fargo said and the door opened. She carried a candle in a low holder, a small, flickering light that nonetheless cast a wide glow, and he saw her eyes move across his smoothly muscled body. Madge halted at the side of the cot, and he saw she wore a thin cotton nightgown, a square neck that let him see the top curve of her breasts. She lowered herself to sit at the edge of the cot.

"I know you're wondering why I can't be more open about being grateful, more demonstrative, shall we say," she began, and he interrupted her.

"Your words, honey, not mine," he said.

"Most men would expect that," she said.

"I'm not most men."

"No, I'm becoming aware of that. I'm very attracted to you. It's just that there are things in the way."

"Things named Terence?" he offered with a smile.

"I haven't changed how I feel about what you're having him do. I'm very afraid of it. I guess it's kind of a wall between us," Madge said. "And I'm sorry for that."

"That makes two of us," Fargo said mildly.

"I wanted you to understand. I want to be honest."

"I appreciate that," he said. "And walls can come down."

"Yes, they can," she said thoughtfully, a tiny furrow on her forehead. She leaned forward suddenly, and her lips pressed his forehead and he felt the softness of her breasts against him for an instant, and then she was standing, hurrying from the room without a backward glance. Alone Fargo half smiled into the darkness. Was there more than just concern over a young man's life, he wondered. Terence Noonan had a dark handsomeness that would reach most women. Had Madge Downey been taken with him? Had she contemplated more than an employer/employee relationship? It hadn't gone further than contemplation for her, Fargo felt reasonably certain. Their exchanges had convinced him that she was still holding herself in. No matter, he'd not be calling back Terence to protect a budding affair, that was certain. She'd have to accept that. He shut off further speculation, closed his eyes, and wrapped sleep around himself.

When morning came he found Madge already up and in the living room, adjusting the loom. "Some quilt making today?" he asked.

"No, just seeing that my yarn is in good shape. I won't start making my quilts till the nights grow longer," Madge said. "Will you come back tomorrow and tell me if you met with Terence?"

"I will," he agreed. "Thanks for the bed and board."

"Thank you for understanding," she said and stepped close to him.

"I'm trying. I'm not sure that I do, though," Fargo said.

"Keep trying," she said and brushed his cheek with her lips, a fleeting instant of softness, and quickly stepped away. He left with her slender body in his mind, the long curve of breasts and legs unhidden by the cotton shirt and the black skirt. He went to the barn, saddled the Ovaro, and rode from Madge's place to the lake where he let the horse drink and stand in the cool water up to his ankles. When he rode on, he paid short visits to the others as he circled the lake.

"Got my cousin and two of his boys arriving in a few days," John Otis told him. "They'll be here with me, waiting for your orders."

"Good," Fargo said and rode on to where he saw Ted Olson standing at the edge of one of his long poultry courses.

"Uncle Zeb and Uncle Ed will be arriving tomorrow," Olson told him. Fargo voiced his appreciation and found much the same news at every place he halted. It was beginning to seem as if there'd be at least a dozen additional men, and he was more and more beginning to think they might well be needed. Joseph Barry was plainly preparing a force for something. Maybe Terence would supply the answer at midnight, Fargo murmured to himself, and by the time he had completed his visiting, the day was at an end. He halted beneath a cottonwood and ate some jerky from his saddlebag, and when the moon rose high, he carefully made his way to the two maples at the north end of Moon Lake.

He pulled the Ovaro into the deepest shadows, dismounted, and sat down to wait. His eyes followed the moon as it crossed the blue velvet cloth that was the sky, and the pale sphere had moved past the high midnight mark when he saw the horseman moving toward him. Fargo rose, his hand on the butt of the Colt at his side as the horseman approached at a fast canter and pulled to a halt at the two trees. Fargo stepped into sight as he saw Terence Noonan's handsome countenance.

"Have any trouble getting here?" he asked.

"No, they close down by ten usually," Terence said. "I'm in solid, did Barry a few personal favors. I saw you bring those two idiots back to him. I was watching from alongside the house. Barry was real mad at them because they acted on their own. Docked them each a week's pay."

"What else have you found out?" Fargo queried.

"I don't know the big plan or anything about it. But they're going to hit at somebody tomorrow night. Barry's real clever. He uses a code name so nobody will actually know anything until they strike. And that way, nobody can let something slip in town," Terence explained.

"What's the code name for this?" Fargo frowned.

"Tamworth," Terence said, and Fargo's frown deepened.

"What the hell does that mean?" he growled.

"I don't know." The younger man shrugged. "But unless you can find out, somebody else is, in Joe Barry's words, going to the poorhouse."

"Tamworth," Fargo repeated. "Doesn't mean a damn thing to me."

"That's all I know," Terence said.

"You've done real well," Fargo said. "Keep watching and listening. I'll be here, same time, two nights from now."

"I'll make it if I can," Terence said and rode away with a wave. Fargo stayed till he was out of sight and decided to bed down where he was. He set out his bedroll, lay back, and wracked his mind over the name Terence had left with him. He reached back into his memory, tried to associate the name with something else, explored all the dusty avenues of past experiences, and finally fell asleep exhausted and frustrated.

When morning came he washed in the lake and finally rode to Madge where she rushed out to meet him. "Did Terence come?" she asked at once.

"Yes," he told her and saw the waiting in her eyes. "He had some things to tell me," he added.

"Don't be mysterious with me, Fargo. I think I've a right to know," she said stiffly.

"Maybe so," he conceded. "The name Tamworth mean anything to you?"

She thought for a moment. "No, nothing," she said finally. "How did he look? Was he all right?"

"He was fine and that's not the top thing on my list for now," Fargo said and knew he'd sounded more annoyed than he intended. Yet he didn't soften the remark, inwardly admitting he was irritated. "Keep that name to yourself," he said. "Unless you think of what it means. Then come get me."

"Where?" Madge asked.

"I'll be at Doc Elton's later today," he said and rode on, realizing he was still annoyed. The only thing she'd really thought about was how Terence looked. He rode the lakeside, peering at everything, trying to find something to connect with the name.

The day had grown late when he reached Doc Elton's office. He entered feeling angry and stymied, and Doc Elton saw his black mood at once and brought out the whiskey. In between sips he told Doc of his meeting with Terence Noonan and the cryptic name Terence had given him.

"Tamworth, you said?" Doc Elton frowned. "I know that name."

Fargo downed the whiskey and leaned forward in his chair, excitement clutching at him.

"My father used to raise Tamworths back in Wales before he brought his family here," Doc continued. "Tamworth's a breed of hog, originating, I think, in Yorkshire. Tamworths are highly regarded by some because they have a skin pigmentation that resists the sun."

"A breed of hog," Fargo murmured as his mind raced. "Orville Dent raises hogs."

Doc Elton's face grew ashen. "That's right, by God."

Fargo leaped to his feet and was halfway out the door and into the night when Doc Elton called after him. "Get some help, Fargo."

"No time for that. They might hit early. I've got to get to Orville Dent's place," Fargo threw back as he vaulted onto the Ovaro and sent the horse into an instant gallop. He raced into the night, headed north to Moon Lake, and made a circle when he came in sight of Orville Dent's place. He rode into the trees and halted where he had a view of the pigpens and feed troughs that stretched out on one side and behind the house. He dismounted and took the big Sharps from its saddle holster. Then he crept forward through the tree cover and dropped to one knee when he was but a few dozen yards from the posthole fence. The house was dark and silent, and he crouched low beside the fence, his eyes sweeping the land beyond.

He had waited perhaps an hour, he guessed, when he saw the figures moving past the house, six of them on foot. Four were carrying small sacks, and all clambered silently through the fence and into the pigpens. They hurried to the four troughs, pulled their sacks open and began dumping the contents into the feed bins. Fargo bent low, slipped through the fence, crept another dozen yards forward, and then dropped to the ground. He brought the rifle to his shoulder as he lay flattened. The two men emptying their sacks into the trough stepped back and another came forward with a pole and stirred the contents of the trough.

Fargo's lips drew back as he aimed. The odds were bad, very bad. He wasn't one for shooting a man in cold blood, but he knew he could afford only one warning, and he lifted his voice. "Drop your guns," he ordered. But as he expected, the figures whirled, each one reaching for a six-gun. Fargo fired the big Sharps and two of the figures beside the nearest trough went down. He fired a third shot and another man fell, half into one of the troughs. The others were shooting back but wildly, trying to fix on their target and Fargo rolled, came up against the fence, and fired off two more shots. Another of the men pitched to the ground, and he saw the remaining two turn and race away. He rose to one knee, drew the Colt and fired at one of the fleeing figures. The man yelped in pain and clutched at his shoulder as he fell, rolled, and managed to squeeze under the rail of the fence.

He was only a rolling blur in the pale darkness so Fargo decided against wasting another bullet. He rose and heard the sound of two horses galloping away as a light went on in the house. The front door of the house pushed open, and he saw Orville Dent emerge in a crouch, a bathrobe wrapped around his bare-legged shape.

"It's me . . . Fargo, over here," Fargo called out and walked forward to see Orville lower the rifle in his hands.

"What in tarnation's goin' on here?" Dent said as he stared at the figures scattered on the ground.

"I found out you were the next target but too late to tell you," Fargo said, and Orville followed him as he strode to where two of the mostly emptied sacks lay on the ground. "They were pouring whatever they had in these sacks into your feed troughs," he said, and Orville took the sack from him and put his nose into it.

"Ground monkshood root," Orville said and made a sour face as he pulled back.

"Poison," Fargo grunted as Sarah Dent came from the house.

"Deadly. Mixed in with the feed, the hogs would have swilled it down. It would've wiped out every one of them," Orville said.

"And pretty much put you in the poorhouse," Fargo added.

"That's for sure," Orville said. "I don't have the money to replace them, or the bank credit to get it. I'd be folding up."

"Which would give Joseph Barry another piece of land to acquire," Fargo said.

"He was behind this?"

"He was, but we can't call him on it, not yet," Fargo said. "But he failed and that's the important thing."

"Yes, I can clean the troughs out with water and put in new, clean feed come morning. I'm real indebted to you, Fargo," Orville Dent said.

"I'll send Ed Brumby to see to these varmints," Fargo said.

"Much obliged. It'll save me the ride to town. Sarah and I want to give the troughs a good cleaning."

Fargo returned to where he'd left the Ovaro and rode slowly back to town. Two of Barry's men had gotten away. They'd tell him what had happened and who had made it happen He'd be more than frustrated. He'd be furious, aware that any direct retaliation would be admitting guilt. But he'd try to find a way, Fargo was certain, and he rode deep into a stand of bur oak as dawn began to peer over the distant hills. He took down his bedroll and stretched out in the cool shade of the forest. He slept soundly until the morning neared noon. When he'd dressed he rode back for another visit to Orville's place where everything looked normal. John Otis and Sam Foreman were there, and they came outside with Orville.

"Mighty fine work last night," John Otis said. "But I'm more worried than ever. Barry will try again and again. You can't be ready each time."

"I'm going to try to be," Fargo said.

"When my cousins come day after tomorrow, we'll have some forty men in all," Sam Foreman said. "That's what you wanted. What do you plan on doing?"

"Keep them waiting and ready until we learn what's behind Joe Barry's moves. That'll depend a lot on what Terence can find out," Fargo said.

"I'm thinking we shouldn't wait too long. Maybe we should just do some raiding of our own," Sam Foreman muttered.

"That could get a lot of people killed and still leave you without answers. We wait some more for now," Fargo said.

"You're running the show. We took you on to do that," Orville Dent put in with gratefulness in his voice. The other two men nodded, Foreman with some reluctance.

"I'll be in touch," Fargo said as he rode on and circled the lake, drawing friendly waves as he did. Word of the night's events had traveled fast. He paused at Madge's place, and she came out to see him, a light blue shirt with three buttons opened at the neck revealing the slow curve of tanned, smooth skin. "I heard," she said. "When do you hope to see Terence again?"

"Tonight," he said.

"Please tell him to be careful. Tell him I'm still afraid for him."

"If there's time. I'm not meeting him to deliver messages," Fargo said, annoyed that he felt so annoyed. She picked up on his answer at once.

"I haven't changed my feelings about his being there," she said.

"I know. It's just that that seems your major concern when you ought to be concerned over the big picture," Fargo said.

She shrugged. "My fault," she said, admittance without concession. "I won't be here all day tomorrow. I'm going to visit Clara Carter. She's some ten miles south of Duchess. She wants some help with her quilt making."

"I'll stop by when I can,' he said more curtly than he'd intended as he wheeled the Ovaro to ride away.

"You be careful, too, Fargo."

He heard her call after him, and there was only sincerity in her voice. He rode on thinking that she had probably developed a real, unfulfilled love for young Terence, and he felt a surge of sympathy for her. The day began to fade and he rode along a ridge, slowing when he spotted five riders below, Barry's son Seth in the lead. They were coming from the direction of Moonside, and he allowed a small smile. They'd probably been there to settle up with Ed Brumby for his grim work. He watched them disappear toward the Barry ranch, and he turned the Ovaro north as night descended.

The moon had begun its climb through the sky when he reached the two maples, stretched out, chewed on some jerky, and let himself doze. When he snapped awake for the third time, the moon was high in the midnight sky, and he rose and scanned the darkness. Perhaps another half hour passed when he spotted the rider moving toward him, and he stepped out as Terence Noonan took form.

The younger man halted and slid from his horse. "Barry's real mad about what happened at the Dent place. He thinks it was just plain luck on your part to be there."

"Learn anything about why he's after all the others?" Fargo queried.

"No, he doesn't ever talk about that, and I've been asking around. I don't think any of his hands know, either. I'd guess only Seth and Jed know," Terence said. "But he's going to hit another tomorrow night. Code name is 'Bee.' "

"Bee?" Fargo frowned.

"That's right. Like all the others, the men assigned to the operation know it only by the code name. Nobody knows what that means until an hour before they set out," Terence said. "You figured out Tamworth. Hope you can do the same with Bee."

"Doc Elton clued me onto Tamworth," Fargo said as Terence climbed onto his horse.

"I don't know if I can meet again so soon. It's too risky without more time in between," Terence said.

"Four nights from now. Think you can make that?" Fargo questioned.

"Yes. That'll give me a few days to make sure Barry's sons see me around. They do the nighttime checking," Terence said.

"Keep your ears open. Try to find out what this is all about, why Barry's after the others. That's still the heart of it," Fargo said and Terence nodded. "Madge said to tell you to be careful and that she's thinking about you," Fargo added.

"Tell her I'm fine." Terence put the horse into a canter. Fargo stayed beneath the maples until he was out of sight and then took the Ovaro and climbed into a low hill and bedded down in a thicket of shadbush. He slept until morning and woke with the code name revolving in his head. "Bee," he murmured aloud. It meant as little as Tamworth had, and he could make no connection with anyone. He dressed and rode toward Moonside, circling the lake. Madge's place was silent as he passed, and he remembered she'd said she'd be visiting for the day. When he reached Doc Elton's office, he had to wait for two hours for the doctor to return before he sat across from him in the small office.

"Got another one for you, Doc," he said. "Bee."

Doc Elton made a face. "Bee?"

"That's the code name, and they're going to hit again tonight," Fargo said. "Anybody around the lake keep bees?"

"No," the doctor said.

"Anyone sell honey? Put up jars of honey for themselves?"

"No, nobody's into that," Doc said.

"A bee pollinates flowers. Any of the womenfolk into flower gardens?" Fargo questioned.

"No. May Otis has a few rose bushes but that's all. Doesn't seem enough to warrant that code name."

"No, it doesn't. I'll set it aside, but I won't rule it out yet," Fargo said. "The damn code name has to tie in with someone or something."

Doc Elton rose and went to scan the wall of books, finally pulled out one volume and, blowing dust from it, handed it to Fargo. "I've got to pay a house call on Emma Tadgett, won't be back till dark. But here's a book on the bee I've kept ever since my school days when we studied bees. Look it over. Maybe it'll trigger something for you."

Fargo took the book and sat back in the chair as Doc Elton hurried from the office. The volume was densely packed despite its slenderness. As Fargo read, the hours went by and his frustration mounted. He had just closed the last page of the book when Doc Elton reappeared. "I put the lamp on two hours ago," Fargo said.

"I was delayed. That always happens when I pay a visit to Emma Tadgett," Doc Elton said. "You've not come up with anything or you wouldn't be here."

"Bull's-eye," Fargo said. "I've learned more about the bee than I ever wanted to know. I've learned that a queen bee can lay three thousand eggs a day and can control a horde of eighty thousand bees. I know how they carry pollen in the stiff hairs of their legs, and they belong to the scientific family of *hymenoptera*. I know everything except what the hell the code name means."

"All the time I was at Emma's I was thinking. Didn't come up with a damn thing, either," Doc said. "What do we do, just sit here wrestling with it while they strike?"

"Got any better ideas?" Fargo asked, and Doc Elton slumped into a chair, his answer the discouragement in his face. "I used to think a bee is a bee. Not anymore. There are four main kinds of bees. I tried to draw some connection between each kind and the small ranchers and came up empty," Fargo said.

"Yes, let's see if I still remember," Doc Elton said. There are bumblebees, honeybees, leaf-cutting bees, and sweat bees."

"Good memory," Fargo said.

Doc Elton smiled ruefully "Only one I left out is the quilting bee, and I'm afraid that doesn't count."

Fargo nodded, then felt the frown touch his brow as Doc's words exploded inside him. "Jesus," he gasped. "Yes, it counts. It's the only damn one that does count." He halted and saw Doc Elton staring back. "A quilting bee. Who makes quilts, dammit?" Fargo almost shouted and saw Doc's jaw drop.

"Madge Downey," Doc breathed as Fargo bolted from the door and vaulted onto the pinto. He had the horse in a gallop in a split second as he raced north toward Moon Lake. He rode hard, stayed on a straight path, and only swerved to the side as he neared Madge's place. He circled and approached from the right, halting to drop out of the saddle and go on foot. He was almost at the house when he spied the six figures, also on foot, moving from the other side toward the house.

Fargo stayed in a crouch, hurried to the rear of the house, and saw the window partly open. He reached it, peered in, and saw the darkened room with the large bed in the center. He glimpsed the dark blond hair against the pillow, the rest of her underneath a large quilt, appropriately enough, Fargo noted in passing. He braced both hands under the window and lifted, inching the window upward. He didn't want Madge to wake and scream in sudden fright. The others were at the front of the house by now, more than close enough to hear a scream. With the window opened enough, he climbed into the room, pulling his long legs over the window sill. Moving on his toes, he was beside the bed in three strides.

He reached down and closed one hand over Madge Downey's mouth and saw her eyes snap open at once. Her scream was an automatic reaction, but his hand stifled the sound, and it took a moment for her to focus and recognize him. "Don't talk. Don't make a sound," he said as he drew back his hand. Madge sat up, the top of her nightgown open, and one long breast almost spilled out. "Get under the bed," Fargo said, "quick." She swung her legs from the bed as he pulled the quilt back, and he pressed her rear down with one hand as she wriggled under the bed, a nice feel to it, firm yet soft, he noted. As soon as she was under the bed, he dived into the spot where she'd been but drew the big quilt entirely over his head.

He lay on his back under the cover, the Colt in his hand, and in moments he picked up the soft sound of the door being opened. They had come in the front of the house, as he'd expected. He lay still, his ears twitching with the approach of the men. Two sets of footsteps, he counted, and a third coming up behind. He was ready, his finger on the trigger of the Colt as a hand ripped the quilt away. "Wake up, honey," the voice said and followed with a curse of surprise.

The next sound that filled the room was the Colt exploding in three shots, so fast they almost seemed one. The figure still holding onto the quilt flew backward in a shower of red, and the man beside him half spun around as the bullet tore through his hip. Fargo's third shot caught the last of the three as he started to go backward, and the impact sent him flying through the door with a spurt of blood erupting from his chest. Fargo whirled and flung himself from the bed as two shots tore into the mattress. He saw a man at the window. He hit the floor, fired, and the man screamed for a brief instant as he threw both hands to his face and then disappeared from sight below the windowsill.

Fargo rose to his feet and heard sounds of footsteps racing across the grounds, then the pounding of hooves in flight. He took a moment to reload, holstered the gun, and dropped to one knee. "Come on out and join the party," he said to the figure flattened under the bed and reached in and helped pull Madge out.

She fell against him, clinging to him, all soft firmness, her breath coming in deep gasps. "My God. Oh, my God," she whispered into his chest, and his hand held the strong curve of her back until she finally pulled away, quickly buttoning the top of the nightgown. "How did you know? How did you get here in time?" she asked.

"I almost didn't," he told her. "Terence gave me a code name. I was lucky enough to figure it out, with some help from Doc Elton."

"Then I owe both you and Terence my life," she said and reached up and kissed his cheek. "I'm eternally grateful."

"But the walls are still there." He smiled.

She took a moment to answer. "I'm afraid yes," she said and there was regret in her face.

"I'll send Ed Brumby back," Fargo said.

"I can't stay here with them lying in my house. I'll go with you." He shrugged and stepped over one of the bodies as he left the room. He waited outside and she emerged in moments, pushing a dark green shirt into denim riding britches. She rode into town with him in silence and stayed in the saddle as he fetched Ed Brumby. The man, wakened, came out in a frayed robe and longjohns and nodded solemnly as Fargo finished.

"I'll get Mike and Sid," Brumby said.

"I ought to get a commission," Fargo observed. "All the business I'm giving you."

"You are that, but I'd keep looking back, mister," the undertaker said.

"Meaning what?"

"Barry's been spouting off in the saloon about how nobody needs a troublemaker like you around," the man said.

"He's right." Fargo smiled and moved to wait beside Madge until Brumby took his one-horse utility wagon from the shed. Fargo turned to Madge who met his eyes, her lovely face still and serious. "Terence is a lucky young man. I'm not sure he knows it."

"Why do you say that?" Madge questioned.

"Having you care so much about what happens to him," Fargo answered.

"I care what happens to you, too, Fargo."

"Differently," he said and smiled.

"Yes, differently," she agreed and nudged her horse after Ed Brumby's wagon. He watched her go and was about to move on past Doc Elton's house when he saw the light on, and he went to the door. Doc Elton answered in slippers and robe, a lamp in his hand. "I was sleeping in my chair, waiting for you to come back. Maybe hoping is a better word," Doc said as Fargo entered and quickly recounted what had taken place. "You're alive and so is Madge. That's all that matters. Spend the rest of the night here. Get yourself some rest. You've earned it."

"Don't mind if I do," Fargo said and after he unsaddled the Ovaro, he collapsed onto the spare bed in Doc's sanatorium. He slept quickly, grateful that things had turned out as they had and aware how close tragedy had come. When he woke in the morning, he had a deep anger burning inside him. He found that Doc Elton had left on an early call, and he saddled the Ovaro with the anger still hard inside him. He had coffee and a muffin out of Doc's kitchen and then rode the pinto northward, skirting Moon Lake to ride to the Barry ranch. It was time to rub Barry's nose in it, perhaps push him into making a mistake. Besides he had developed an active hate for the man and his tactics, ruthless and clever as they were.

Joseph Barry stepped from his house, Seth and Jed beside him as Fargo came to a halt. "What do you want here, Fargo?" Joseph Barry snapped, his face set in stone.

"I thought you were going to keep a tighter rein on your hands," Fargo said.

"That's my problem," Barry said.

"Not when they're trying to kill friends of mine," Fargo said.

"You accusing me of something?" Joseph Barry glared. "I told you the boys go their own way sometimes."

"I'm saying they better stop," Fargo answered. "I'm holding you to see that they do."

He enjoyed seeing Joseph Barry's face turn dark

red as the man stifled his fury. "You're asking for real trouble, Fargo," the man said.

"My middle name," Fargo said. "You just remember what I said."

"You remember what *I* said," the man flung back as Fargo turned the horse and rode away. The Barrys couldn't see the tight smile that touched his lips. It was a dangerous game he'd decided to play, but Joseph Barry was ready to be pushed into a mistake, a mistake that might make him reveal why he wanted to get rid of all the ranchers around Moon Lake. With Terence inside, that final question might be answered. He had made Barry take the bait once before. Maybe he could do it again.

5

Fargo had ridden the Lake Moon area for most of the day, formulating the other plans he'd decided to pursue when he returned to Doc Elton's at dusk. "Got a message for you," Doc said. "Jed Berry stopped by and said he'd be waiting to meet with you at the saloon at eight o'clock. He said he'd a plan for how you and his pa could work together."

Fargo lifted one brow and his lips pursed. "You believe that?" he asked.

"Can't say I do. The Barrys aren't ones for compromising, none of them."

"The little bastard probably figures to take me down," Fargo said.

"Isn't the saloon a little public for murdering a man?" Doc asked.

"Not when you can fix it to look like a gunfight," Fargo said.

"You figure that's what he wants to do?"

"One way or another."

"Then you won't go," Doc said.

"No, I'll be there," Fargo said.

"Why would you want to go get yourself killed," Doc Elton said in exasperation.

"I don't aim to let that happen."

"Hell, you just said he can fix it his way."

"Except for one thing," Fargo said. "He'll think I've come to hear what he has to say, but I'll be ready and waiting for his first move. I expect that'll give me thirty seconds on him."

"I still say you're walking on thin ice, my friend," Doc Elton said.

"Been on thin ice before, Doc," Fargo said. "Barry's hurting. If I can hurt him more he'll make a mistake."

"God, be careful. You're holding a lot of people's hopes," Doc said as he walked Fargo to the door and watched the big man swing onto the pinto.

Fargo waved back as he rode slowly away. He had at least an hour before the eight o'clock time Jed Barry had set, but that was what he needed. He wanted to survey the saloon with an eye for survival, and when he reached the building, he saw that the night's customers were already crowding in. He entered, took a small table near the wall, and ordered a bourbon from one of the waitresses letting his eyes scan the room as he sipped the drink.

A row of kerosene lamps behind the bar afforded the light for the bar area. The rest of the saloon was illuminated by a big Conestoga wagon wheel suspended from the ceiling with candles and kerosene lamps attached to it. The entire chandelier was held in place by a stout length of hemp that hung from a ceiling beam. Fargo studied the fixture for another few minutes before he let his eyes roam across the room again. He took note of a small, square wooden table at the back edge of the half circle of tables, and his eyes went back to the chandelier again for a moment as he measured angles and distances. Satisfied, he leaned back and watched the customers continue to line up at the bar. Perhaps his precautions wouldn't be needed, he admitted to himself. But he'd not be laying his life on that possibility.

A few minutes past eight o'clock he saw Jed Barry enter, his smallish figure bristling with the tensed-wire chemistry that was built into him. Fargo rose as the man halted, and he saw the five other men come in behind Jed Barry. Fargo walked slowly forward toward the center of the floor where Barry waited, a sneer on his face. Out of his peripheral vision, Fargo saw the other five men spread out on each side of Jed Barry to form a half circle, and he smiled inwardly. Barry had no intention of talking about how they could work together.

"You wanted to say something to me," Fargo began. "I'm here to listen."

"I've something to tell you, all right. It's that you're a goddamn yellow-backed, no-good bastard," Jed Barry said.

Fargo heard the silence settle over the saloon and caught the figures starting to move away, back toward the door and the walls. "Your pa send you to say that, sonny?" Fargo asked mildly.

Jed Barry's eyes narrowed at once. "Don't call me sonny," he rasped.

"You didn't answer me, sonny. Your pa send you?" Fargo said.

"No, goddammit. I'm here on my own," Barry almost shouted. "I'm going to give you a chance to draw on me, big man, unless you're too yellow."

Fargo started to back away from the younger man slowly. Jed Barry held his place in the center of the floor, four of his men also well under the circle of the wagon wheel chandelier. "I didn't come here for a gunfight," Fargo said.

"You see, he is a yellow-back," Jed called out with a sneer. "You draw or I'll gun you down," he said to Fargo.

"Now I came here to talk. You said you wanted to talk," Fargo answered as he continued to slide backward. He was almost opposite the wooden table as he edged a step closer.

"I changed my mind. Draw, damn you," the youth snarled.

Fargo's glance flicked to the other five men. When Jed Barry drew they'd all draw, and some of their shots would certainly hit him. In his conceit Jed Barry believed he could outdraw him and the others were just insurance. The youth was very wrong, but to prove that meant taking at least two bullets, too high a price to pay for teaching a punk a fatal lesson. Fargo took a last step backward. It brought him just behind the square table. It was time to put precautions into practice.

He dived, flinging himself sideways as he up-ended the table with one motion and was already behind the thick wood as Jed Barry and the others drew their guns. Their bullets began to slam into the wall and the table, but Fargo was prepared and fired only one shot from behind his barricade. The bullet hurtled into the length of hemp holding the chandelier, and he saw the strands of rope come apart. Split seconds later the heavy wagon wheel chandelier crashed down, landing directly on Jed Barry and two of his men, plunging most of the room into darkness as candles and kerosene lamps sputtered out.

But the lamps behind the bar offered some light,

and Fargo half rose and saw two of Jed Barry's men rushing to the shattered Conestoga wheel. He fired and both went down, their bodies draping over the wheel spokes. He whirled and glimpsed the fifth man trying to flee. He took aim, fired as the man started to run into the darkness, and saw the figure pitch forward to lay still, spread-eagle on the floor. Fargo straightened up and stepped forward. A half dozen men stopped cowering against the base of the bar and came forward to lift the wagon wheel. Jed Barry's head seemed to have been driven halfway through his neck, his lifeless form crumpled on the floor. His two gunhands lay with their necks pierced by pieces of shattered spokes.

Fargo holstered his gun. "The best laid plans . . ." he observed and walked slowly from the saloon as others made way for him. Outside he pulled himself onto the Ovaro and unhurriedly returned to Doc Elton.

"You're a sight for sore eyes," Doc said. "But still it was a damfool thing to do."

"No argument there," Fargo said. "But Barry's getting one of his sons back dead. He'll be really shaken now. Let's see what he does."

Fargo took advantage of another night in bed at Doc's sanatorium, and he slept late. When he rode out he moved north toward Moon Lake, stayed in tree cover, and saw pairs of riders sweeping up and down the rolling countryside. They were plainly searching for him, and he walked the pinto through a thick stand of quaking aspen. Near the end of the stand he'd seen four pairs of riders racing back and forth. He halted as Joseph Barry suddenly appeared on a black gelding, two of his men with him, and the man halted as two pairs of the searchers reported to him. Fargo dismounted and pulled the Sharps from its saddle holster. He made his way forward on foot, almost to the edge of the tree cover. Joseph Barry was close enough for him to hear now.

"I want that bastard. Find him, dammit," the man demanded.

"We've been searchin' all morning, boss," one of the men said. "Maybe he ran."

"That's shit. He didn't run, damn him. He's around here someplace," Barry thundered.

Fargo raised the rifle to his shoulder, aimed, and fired, and the hat flew from Joseph Barry's head. "You're right," Fargo called from the trees as Barry froze in place and the others seemed unsure what to do.

"Goddamn you," Barry rasped.

"That could've been *your* head," Fargo said. The man glared at the line of trees, but he didn't move, all too aware of the truth in Fargo's words. "Your boy lied about wanting to talk to me. He came to kill me. Everybody in the saloon knows that. Maybe they won't say it to your face but they know it."

"You expect me to believe that?" Barry shouted.

"I do, because you know it's true, not that I give a damn whether you believe it or not," Fargo said.

"You're a goddamn fool, Fargo. I can send my men in there after you and you're dead, and I've others nearby," Barry called.

"Do it and it'll be your last order," Fargo said and saw Barry's lips twitch in frustration and rage.

"You shoot me and they'll all go after you. They'll run you down," the man said, but Fargo caught the edge of bluster in his voice.

"Maybe, but you won't be alive to see it," Fargo said. "Your move, mister."

Barry stared into the trees for another long moment and then backed his horse. "It's not finished, Fargo, not till you're a dead man," he called as he turned the horse and started away, the others following him. Fargo waited till they were well away before he rode from the aspen, the rifle still in one hand. There wasn't a lot left of the day, and he settled into a thicket of shadbush and let himself doze until he woke with the night on the land. He rose refreshed, his own plans calling for a sleepless night watching the outskirts of the Barry place.

He'd be keeping his meetings with Terence, of course, but they were no longer enough. The climate had changed. Joseph Barry was hurt and enraged enough to do the unexpected, perhaps advancing his timetable, perhaps something else might reveal his reasons for his vendetta against the small landholders around the lake. Fargo walked the pinto to a small rise where a line of hackberry let him watch unseen, the Barry ranch spread out just below him, the outskirts reaching out to the base of the rise. He watched as the lights went out in the bunkhouses and then, later, in the main house, and the ranch settled into silence. It seemed plain that there'd be no activity out of Barry this night. Yet Fargo held his place, determined not to take anything for granted.

He relaxed as the hours went by and listened to the distant call of the coyotes and the high-pitched angry cries of kit foxes in a squabble. Another quiet hour had gone by when he suddenly caught the movement near the outskirts of the ranch. He edged forward, peered through the pale moonlight, and saw the horse and rider moving slowly along a line of hawthorns. The horseman moved closer, and Fargo saw he wore a long, black duster and a wide-brimmed black Stetson that covered him completely. Frowning, Fargo watched the horseman halt and wait, and a few minutes later he saw another figure, this one on foot, running in a crouch from the Barry ranch. Fargo stayed motionless, watching as the figure on foot rounded the line of hawthorns and, with a stab of surprise, he recognized Terence Noonan.

Terence stopped beside the horseman in the black duster, and they spoke in soft, whispered exchanges he couldn't hear. They spoke for perhaps five minutes, and then Terence Noonan made his way back to the ranch, again running in a crouch. The horseman, a cadaverous, black figure, turned and rode back the way he had come. Fargo spurred the Ovaro through the hackberry, caught up to the horseman below, paralleled the rider and then, as the figure moved onto more open ground, he swung in behind. The horseman increased speed, and Fargo turned the Ovaro to climb a low hill. He stayed at a fast canter through a row of Rocky Mountain maples and then turned down the slope to halt as the horseman approached.

The Colt in his hand, he faced the black-shrouded rider. "That's far enough," he growled. "What business did you have with Terence Noonan?"

The horseman moved a few paces closer and Fargo raised the Colt. "You can put that down," the rider said and whipped off the wide-brimmed black Stetson, and Fargo saw the dark blond hair cascade down.

"Damn," he gasped out. "Damn." He heard

himself almost sputter as he groped for words. "The question holds," he said finally. "You've some answering to do."

"At my place," she said and moved her horse forward as he swung in beside her. He rode in silence, thoughts whirling inside him. Her concern for Terence Noonan suddenly had a new dimension. He had concluded she had developed a real, unfulfilled love for the young man. Maybe he'd been very wrong. Maybe it hadn't been unfulfilled he mused as they came in sight of her house. She stabled the horse as he dismounted and waited, and when she returned she took off the long, black duster. He followed her into the house where she turned to face him, a light cotton blouse resting on the long curve of her breasts, her wide face held in tightly. "You're thinking wrong things," Madge said.

"Prove it," Fargo said stiffly.

"Terence is more than a hired hand," she said.

"I'd already figured that much out," Fargo returned.

"He's my brother," she said simply, and Fargo knew his jaw had dropped open. He watched Madge lower herself onto the edge of the settee, and he sat down beside her. 'Terence was running with a bad crowd, and he was caught and sentenced to jail. He served his time and came to me when he got out. I needed someone so we invented the hired-hand story. Folks here were so nervous and on edge with all that was going on, we thought it'd make them more nervous if they knew an ex-jailbird was working here," she explained.

"I'd feel better if you'd told me the truth," Fargo said.

"Didn't see it made any difference." Madge

shrugged. "But I knew what you were thinking. I just couldn't tell you how wrong you were." She leaned forward and suddenly her lips were on his, soft and warm, holding for a long moment. But as he began to press his mouth on hers, she drew away.

"I thought maybe walls were coming down," Fargo said.

"Some," she said.

"But not enough."

"I still don't like what you're having Terence do. I'm afraid for him. That wall is still there," she said.

"Too bad," Fargo remarked.

"Yes," she agreed gravely. "I'm sorry, too."

"Work on it," he said and her hand came to rest on his.

"Don't tell the others. It won't help anyone or anything," she pleaded, and he thought for a moment and found himself agreeing with her. Terence was their inside man. There was nothing to be gained by making the others uncertain about him.

"All right," he said. "For now."

"What's that mean?" She frowned.

"Until he gives me some reason to tell the others."

"He won't. This is Terence's chance to prove himself. That's why he was so quick to volunteer," Madge said.

Fargo nodded. Faith, blood ties, caring—they were powerful forces. He hoped she was right in everything, but he couldn't afford her loyalties. Too many other lives were at stake. "Don't go visiting him again," he said, more sharply than he'd intended. She frowned questioningly. "It's a risk everytime I meet with him. I don't want him taking any other risks," he said as he rose.

"All right," she said, almost contritely and walked from the house with him. "You could stay the night if you like," she said.

"Not tonight," he said.

"Don't trust your self-discipline?"

"Something like that."

"Then trust mine," she said.

He smiled and pulled her to him, pressing his mouth hard on hers, and felt her lips respond. He heard her tiny gasp and then she pulled away. "Still want me to trust yours?" he asked.

"No," she said, shaking her head, the dark yellow hair flying from side to side. He left, swinging into the saddle and saw her hurry back into the house. She wanted to tear walls down, he was certain, but she had her own inner principles and she clung to them. He gave her credit for that as he rode back into the hills with the first dawn light touching the trees.

He found a spot to bed down, deep in a mountain ash thicket, and he slept till noon. He circled the lake when he returned to the saddle, searching the terrain as he rode. Joseph Barry had no more hunting parties out searching for him, and finally he halted atop a hill in a line of hackberry that afforded a view of Barry's ranch. He spotted no unusual activity of any kind, except for too many men lounging around, but he kept watch until the hours slid into the night. He left then and rode to the two maples at the north end of Moon Lake where he settled down and waited as the moon rose to paint a shimmering path across the water.

The night had deepened when he saw Terence

come into sight and approach the twin maples. "Heard about you killing Jed Barry in the saloon," Terence said.

"His fault," Fargo grunted. "What do you have for me?"

"Not much. No code names. He's not planning an attack on anyone right soon, it seems," Terence said. "But he's planning something big. He's replacing six of the men you took out. They're due to arrive tomorrow afternoon. Then there are six more coming the next day and another dozen the day after."

"He's getting ready for an all-out move," Fargo said. "But you can't get a lead on why?"

"Nope. No talk about that. But he has a safe in his study. He and Seth Barry have been taking papers out of it, studying them, and locking them away again. I saw that because he had me doing some repairs inside the main house," Terence said.

"I'd guess maybe the answer I want is in that safe," Fargo murmured. "Maybe you can help me get inside the house."

"Maybe," Terence said.

"But first we have to do something about all these men he's bringing in. With the men he already had, I make a guess he'll have some sixty or so men. That's too many. I've got to cut that down some," Fargo said.

"How?" Terence queried.

"I'll have to think about that. How about we meet three nights from now. I don't want to wait longer than that," Fargo said, and the younger man nodded his agreement. "Madge won't be meeting with you anymore. She told me who you were," Fargo said and Terence Noonan's face darkened.

"Dammit, she wasn't going to tell anybody," he said angrily.

"She had to tell me. I saw her meet you. It's risky enough for you to meet *me*. I don't want you taking more chances than you need to take." Terence Noonan nodded and some of the instant anger went from his face. "Get back and keep listening and watching," Fargo said and stayed in place until Terence rode out of sight in the darkness.

Fargo walked the pinto from the trees, skirted the lake, and finally halted at Orville Dent's place where he woke the hog farmer from his sleep. "Trouble?" Orville frowned, rubbing sleep from his eyes as he faced Fargo in his longjohns.

"Get the others here for a meeting in the morning," Fargo said. "Not all the newcomers, just the regulars."

"All right," Orville said.

"I'll be here by nine," Fargo said and left the man looking perplexed. There was enough of the night left to catch some sleep, and Fargo lay down under the peachleaf willow and slept until morning. He appeared at Orville Dent's by nine, his plans formed. The others were already there, and he quickly recounted what Terence had told him. "Whatever he's planning, we'd best beat him to it," Orville said.

"Maybe we can. First, I want to even the odds some and maybe delay him a few days more while he waits," Fargo said.

"How?" Abe Abelson asked.

"I'll need a good-sized barn first," Fargo said.

"I can give you that," Sam Foreman said.

"Then pick six men to stand guard in six-hour shifts," Fargo said, and the others nodded gravely.

"Get six more men and go to the road that leads to Moon Lake from the south, the one with the stand of box elder on both sides."

"We know the one," Foreman said.

"One of you take the six men and hole up on both sides of that road. When you see me you'll know what to do," Fargo said.

"When?" Foreman queried.

"Be in position by noon. I'm not sure when I'll be along," Fargo said.

"I'll be waiting," Sam Foreman said.

"See you then," Fargo said and hurried from the house. He rode into the rolling hill country and halted to devour a half dozen sweet peaches, then slowly made his way toward the Barry ranch. He turned off before he neared it and climbed a high hill that gave him an eagle's-eye view of the land below in all directions. He relaxed atop the Ovaro and waited.

6

Fargo spotted the thin column of dust first and immediately moved the Ovaro from his hilltop vantage point. He rode downhill at a fast canter as the thin column came closer, cut sideways, and finally saw the horsemen, six riders moving northward in the direction of the Barry ranch. Fargo spurred the pinto across a low hill and halted on the narrow road as the six riders came into sight. They slowed as they came up to him and Fargo offered a friendly smile. "You boys on your way to Joe Barry's place?" he called out.

"That's right," the first one answered out of a long, thin face with meanness stamped on it.

"This way." Fargo smiled again and, with a wave, put the pinto into a trot. The six riders swung after him at once, and he had gone a few thousand yards when the mean-faced man drew alongside him. "You're turning east," he said.

"The boss decided it'd be best if you came in the back way," Fargo said affably as he turned onto the road lined with the box elder. He went another few hundred yards when Sam Foreman and his men burst from both sides of the road, all with guns drawn. Fargo threw up his hands, and the others did the same, instantly aware they were trapped.

Their looks of surprise turned into frowns as, after their guns were taken, Fargo dropped his hands and joined Sam Foremen.

"The barn and the guards are waiting," Foremen said.

"Tie them carefully. We'll do it again tomorrow, same place same time," Fargo said, and Sam Foreman took the six men in single file, a pleased smile on his face. Fargo watched them disappear down the road and turned the Ovaro north again, the day nearing an end when he drew up to Madge's place. She opened the door for him at once, her eyes searching his face. "He's fine," Fargo said and saw her face relax. "I know he's your kid brother, but you can't look out for him forever," he said.

"I just think he's had a bad run of luck. It's been that way all his life with Terence," she said.

"Some people seem to run into bad luck," Fargo said.

"I know." Madge nodded gravely and, shaking off a moment of difficulty, she took his hand. "I've leftover stew that's real tasty. Stay for supper," she said, and he agreed at once. The stew turned out to be everything she'd said, and a shot glass of bourbon added to the pleasures of the table. "What happens after tomorrow?" she asked.

"I'll meet with the others. We'll have to make plans to take on Barry. I'd like knowing why he wants everybody's land. I still think that might help us, but we may not be able to wait," Fargo admitted.

"You've plans made already, haven't you?" Madge said.

"Some," he allowed and drew a wry smile.

"Don't make Terence a part of them," she said. "Bring him out."

"Can't. He is a part of them, a key part."

"Every day he stays at Barry's camp he takes a greater chance of being found out. Hasn't he done enough?" Madge asked.

"He's done real well, but there's one last thing to do or we risk losing too many men and women in trying to hit Joe Barry straight on," Fargo said. She stared into space, her eyes touched by despair. "I'll give Terence a choice. How about that?" Fargo offered.

"He'll agree to stay, of course," Madge said with a touch of reproach. "It'll be one more way for him to redeem himself."

"That's the second time you've talked about him proving himself, redeeming himself," Fargo pointed out as her lips tightened. "Why? He was jailed, served his time and came out. Why does he have to redeem himself?" he questioned sharply.

Madge closed her eyes for a moment as she answered unhappily. "He didn't serve his time. He escaped," she said.

Fargo's jaw grew tight. "Any more little things you haven't told me?" he tossed at her.

"No," she said very softly. 'Does this mean you won't believe anything I say anymore?"

"Let's say I'll think twice," Fargo snapped.

"I can't blame you," she conceded, and as he rose she came to him and her hand pressed his arm. "Don't be angry. Stay the night."

He let thoughts skip through his mind. Her place was convenient to where he had to be tomorrow, and her loyalty to a younger brother was understandable, if perhaps a little overdone. "All right," he said. "I'd be obliged."

"I know you're trying to do the best for everyone and that includes me," she said. "I've just never been able to give Terence the help or support he needed, and I guess I'm feeling a little guilty about that."

"Subject closed," he said. "Good night, Madge."

"Good night," she said, and he made his way to the small room and comfortable cot he'd used before. He undressed and stretched out in the dark, and a sliver of pale light edged its way through the window. He let plans go through his mind again and was unhappy at what seemed to be the need to act too soon. Yet Barry was plainly getting ready for something. What drove the man? That was still the question he wanted answered. Why was Joseph Barry so determined to get rid of everyone around Moon Lake?

The question was still hanging when he heard the door open and saw Madge holding a small candle on a metal carrier. She wore the cotton nightgown hanging loosely, the top unbuttoned as she moved toward him. She set the holder down on the small end table, and the flickering glow cast a soft light as she lowered herself to the edge of the cot. "Thanks for understanding," she murmured.

"Understanding isn't changing," he said.

"I know. I'm still grateful, and for saving my neck the other night," Madge said, and suddenly she was bending over him. He saw the top of one smooth, white breast push up from the neck of the nightgown. Her mouth pressed down on his, gently first, then with greater strength, and he felt her lips working against his.

She pulled back for a moment, and he searched her eyes, suddenly dark and liquid. "Is that what this is? Gratitude?" he asked.

"Yes, but it's good to be grateful and do something you want to do anyway," she said, a half smile edging her lips. As he watched, she leaned back, reached upward, and pulled the nightgown from her. He saw the pleasure in her eyes, almost a trumphant smugness, as she saw him enjoy the loveliness of her. And enjoy it he did, her breasts long yet curving into fullness at the bottoms, each tipped by a red nipple set in the center of a lighter red circle, her rib cage long and narrowing to a small waist and an almost flat abdomen, her skin soft white. She moved her legs and revealed their long, slender lines, her thighs without extra fat yet not without shape, coming together at the very black V of thick, tufted denseness.

He reached his hands out and cupped both breasts as he felt the smoothness of her, and at his touch she uttered a low gasp and stretched out beside him. His mouth found hers, wet and waiting, her lips instantly working hungrily, her tongue a suddenly darting thing that thrust forward and back. His hand caressed the long breasts, slowly moving down their smoothness. His thumb slid gently across each red tip and felt each grow firmer as Madge made soft cooing sounds of delight. He brought his lips down to the right breast, drew in its soft-firm tip, and caressed it with his tongue. Madge cried out, and he felt her body arch upward. "Oh, oh, oooooh," she moaned, and her fingers dug into his shoulders.

As he sucked on each breast, slipping his mouth from one to the other, Madge's body lifted and jerked with tiny spasms of delight. His hand moved down the smoothness of her waist and flat abdomen to push into the dark, dense tuft, and he felt her pubic mound curving upward underneath. Now her long, slender thighs, held tightly together, were falling from one side to the other as she uttered tiny screams of anticipation. His hand pushed in between them and felt the dampness of her skin, moved up to the tufted V again, and suddenly her thighs fell open as the sunflower's petals fall open and he felt her hips push upward.

"Oh, God, yes, Jesus . . . yes, yes," Madge breathed, her voice suddenly hoarse, and he brought his throbbing eagerness atop her as she screamed and her fingers dug into his back. He slid forward and felt her wetness envelope him as she pushed forward again, welcoming and consuming. She uttered long, low moaning sounds as he moved with her in the contact that was unlike any other, and he felt himself surging but held back. Suddenly Madge was screaming, a long, eager paean of fleshy wanting, and her dark tuft was hitting against his groin in short, spasmodic motions. He came with her and felt the world imploding in that single instant until he lay atop her, his long, deep breaths mingling with hers as, her thighs around his hips, she held him inside her.

"God, oh, God," Madge murmured and pulled his head down against her breast, pushing one nipple to rest against his lips. She lay that way until finally her thighs slid down from him and, with a reluctant sigh, she let him slide from her and turned to lay against him, one long breast pressed into his chest. "You were right. Walls can come down," she said.

"For the right reasons, I hope," Fargo said.

"For the right reasons," she said. "You can't be bought, I know that. I'm sure it's been tried often enough."

"Often enough," he said and her eyes held a sudden mischievousness.

"Of course, there's always a first time," she said. "I could try again."

"You could." He nodded.

"I think I will," she said, and he felt her hand reach down and close around him, gently stroking and pulling. His response was instant, and she gave a tiny gasp as she closed her fingers tighter, delight in her voice. His mouth found one breast as she continued to stroke and caress, and then suddenly she was turning her body, bringing her legs over him, opening herself and plunging down onto him. "Ahhhhhh, ah, ah, God, so good, ah," Madge cried out as her hips twisted and rotated to take in all of him. In moments she was bouncing up and down, thrusting and pumping and her head was against his chest as she uttered tiny screams of utter joy.

Suddenly, when he felt her legs tighten against his hips, he spun, carried her with him, and was atop her as she exploded with him, a long cry of delirious pleasure bursting from her. He heard his own half shout of gratification fusing with hers. Finally she lay beside him, one arm across his chest, one long, soft breast against his ribs, and her eyes met his. "Good try," he said blandly.

"I thought so," she murmured as she settled into his arms and quickly slept.

He held her there and closed his eyes until the morning sun slid through the window. She rose, disdaining the nightgown as she walked from the room, and he enjoyed the way her long breasts swayed gently. "I'll get breakfast," she said and vanished out the door as he rose and used the porcelain washbasin. Finally dressed he went into the kitchen where Madge had biscuits and coffee on the table. She'd put on a skirt but nothing more, and he took in the sheer beauty of the way her breasts dipped and rose, swayed and gently bounced as she served breakfast.

"You trying to get me to stay?" he asked.

"Yes."

"I wish I could, but I have to play the role of Judas goat once more," he said. "But I could come back afterward."

"I can wait," she said and bent over, kissed him, and let her breast brush his face.

"You're a damn vixen," he said, and her little laugh was admission. She donned a shirt before he left and watched him ride away from the door as he headed south, back to the high hill that let him survey the land. He waited patiently there, and the day had begun to slide toward an end when he picked up the horsemen, coming from the east this time, six riders moving on their way toward the Barry ranch.

Once again he rode down and intercepted them with the same friendly smile he'd shown the other six. "You the boys Joe Barry's expecting?" he asked and they nodded. "This way," he said with a wave, and the six horsemen followed him as he led them to the road bordered by the hackberry. Halfway through it, John Otis and his men burst into the open and took the six riders prisoner.

"Barry has a dozen more coming tomorrow but

a dozen's too risky. Something goes wrong, and a few get away and Barry will know what happened to the twelve we have. I don't want that. I want him to sit around waiting for them so we'll let the ones tomorrow join him," Fargo said. "Meanwhile, call a meeting for tomorrow. Orville's place as usual."

"See you there," Otis said as they led their captives away and dusk began to settle over the land. Fargo waited and let the night deepen before he returned to Madge's house, turning plans in his mind before he did so. She greeted him with her lips pressing his.

"Everything go well?" she asked, and he nodded.

"I called a meeting tomorrow at Orville's," he said.

"We can go together," she said with a touch of smugness.

Later, when he lay beside her in her bed this time, her gasped breaths of pleasure still hanging in the air, she rose onto one elbow and her eyes studied his face. "You're real quiet," she said. "Something's wrong."

"Wouldn't say that exactly," he said.

"What would you say exactly?" she pressed.

"I'd say I'm not happy about having to move against Joe Barry but he's forcing my hand," Fargo said.

"How?"

"It's damn plain he's getting ready to move against all of you. We can't let him do that. I wanted to try and avoid a pitched battle that'll mean a lot of your people getting killed, too," Fargo said. "I wanted time to find out why he's doing this, and maybe that'd show me a way to get at him."

"As you said, that doesn't seem to be in the cards," Madge said.

"Right, dammit, and I'm not happy having to do what I don't want to do. I just can't see any other way out," Fargo said.

Her hands caressed his face. "Maybe something will turn up yet."

"Nothing wrong with being an optimist," he sniffed and wished he could borrow some of her spirit as he went to sleep with his arms cradling her.

When morning came, Madge rode to Orville Dent's with him where the others were already gathered. He spoke quickly and grimly as he began to outline his plans. "I'd guess we've bought a few more days while Barry waits for the men who won't be arriving," he began. "But I don't know how much more than a few days or just how he's planning to strike. That means we have to do two things."

"Such as?" Lem Carter asked.

"First, make sure that if he does hit first, he won't wipe us out and second, make plans to hit him," Fargo said.

"We've forty some men. Couldn't we stand up to him?"

"And lose over half? That's too high a price. He outguns you," Fargo told them.

"How do you figure to stop him from wiping us out if he attacks first?" John Otis asked.

"We won't be here," Fargo answered and saw the others frown. "There'll be no one here for him to wipe out. Except for Orville, Ted, Abe Abelson, and Madge, the rest of your people will be in the north hills. You'll split them into four groups tonight, and they'll take their guns and provisions for three days. I want them far enough away so's any of Barry's men won't come on them by accident. They'll stay in tree cover during the day, and at night they'll watch for our signal."

"Signal?" Orville questioned.

"That's right. That's where you, Ted, and Abe come in. The others will be far back in the north hills. We're going to have to send the signal in relays," Fargo said. "I'll let Terence pick the night. When Barry's men are asleep in his three bunkhouses and the time's right, Terence will signal with a lantern. I'll be outside Barry's place watching. When I see Terence's signal, I'll light my lantern and wave it. You, Orville, will be halfway to the hills, but close enough to see my signal. You'll signal to Ted, who'll be farther back, and he'll in turn signal with his lantern to Abe, who'll be at the bottom of the north hills."

"When the others see Abe's lantern they come out?" Otis asked.

"That's right, and converge where I'll be waiting nearest to Barry's place, and I'll lead the attack," Fargo said. "You explain it to the others tonight. Tell them to be watching every night. It might take two or three days before Terence has the right night to signal me. Remember, they don't come down until they see the signal."

"Where does Madge fit in?"

"Backup, for any of us. Insurance. You never know," Fargo said.

"Guess not," Orville said.

"You going to leave me out?" Doc Elton asked.

"No, sir. You'll be with the others in the hills

and you'll come down with them. You'll be there to treat the wounded, and I hope you have no work," Fargo said.

"I hope so, too," Doc agreed

"Now get going, talk to all your people and move them into the north hills tonight," Fargo said.

"What about those varmints we're holding?" Sam Foreman asked.

"Tie them hand and foot and leave them. They can go without eating for three days," Fargo said. "Tomorrow night, Orville, Abe, Ted, and Madge will meet here with me, and we'll take up our positions come dark."

The others began to file from the house, their faces grave but determined, and he found Madge beside him as he walked outside. "Thanks for letting me be an important part of it," she said.

"You've earned a place," he said.

"Just how do you mean that?" she said to him, her eyes dancing.

"Not the way you mean, sassy. Now get to your place. I'll see you tomorrow night." He swung onto the Ovaro and rode the hills, circled high above the Barry ranch, and stayed watch till the day moved to a close when he rode to the twin maples at the north end of the lake. Terence arrived after the moon hung high, and Fargo quickly told him of the plans he'd put into effect. "It all hangs on your signal, Terence. Can you do it?"

"Should be no problem," Terence said. "I can easily get hold of a lantern. I'll just be sure and pick the right night when they're all settled in."

"Good," Fargo said.

"Barry's steaming mad at the men he hired who

haven't shown yet. He's giving them another two days."

"Which means we've bought two days. He won't make any moves till the two days are passed. I'll still keep watching him during the days," Fargo said. "And every night."

"Keep watching. I'd guess I won't need more than a night or two," Terence said and rode off with a wave. Fargo thought about riding to Madge but decided the hour had grown late, and he bedded down under a cottonwood. When morning came he returned to Orville's place.

"Sam stopped by. Everyone's in the north hills and spread out, and they all know what to do," Orville said.

"Good. See you come dark," Fargo said and returned to the hills. He rode to the spot that let him look down at the Barry ranch and imprinted the layout of the bunkhouses in his mind. Finally he left and slept some in the dark cool of an oak thicket, and when he rose he moved back to Orville's place as the night descended. The others were there when he arrived, and Orville had a kerosene lantern waiting for him as well as the one for himself. Abe and Ted had their lanterns tied to their lariat straps.

"We'll be moving out," Orville said.

"If nothing happens, we meet here come morning," Fargo said, and the others nodded as they rode off to take up their positions. Alone with Madge, he put an arm around her. "See you in the morning," he said.

"What do you mean? I'm going with you."

"No. I'll watch alone. Less chance of being seen by accident that way," he told her.

"Then why am I here?" she queried.

"I told you, backup, insurance, standby in case something happens to one of us," he said.

"I just sit around here waiting. I don't know that I like that," she protested. "And there's little chance you or the others will be hurt."

"You can't say that. Abe's no spring chicken. He could pull a muscle. Ted Olson already has a limp. Dammit, you want to play a part or don't you?" Fargo snapped, and she tossed him a glower that quickly faded.

"All right, you win," she said and leaned her head against his chest for a moment. "I just hate feeling useless."

"You're not. Now relax and I'll be back in time." He left, but not before her lips clung to his for another moment. The lantern hanging from his saddle horn, he carefully rode to the outskirts of the Barry ranch and closeted himself in a stand of mountain ash that let him see the front section of the ranch. The light stayed on longest in the ranch house, and finally it too went out and only silent darkness enveloped the land. He waited through the night, dismounting to stretch a few times, and saw no glimmer of a lantern being held aloft from below. When the new sun nosed its way over the hills, he backed the pinto from the trees and returned to Orville's place.

Orville and the others returned soon after, their faces showing the effects of sleeplessness. "Everybody turn in. Tomorrow's another night," Fargo said.

"You can sleep in Sarah's bedroom, Madge," Orville said.

"I'll go back to my place and see you tonight," Madge told him and paused beside Fargo.

"I want to sleep," he told her, and she allowed a secret little smile as she walked from the house. He found a spot inside Orville's place to stretch out, undressed, and welcomed sleep. When dusk came, he woke and the others did the same. Orville had coffee and rabbit cooked in an onion sauce ready to eat, and they had just finished the meal when Madge arrived. She brought some tangled skeins of yarn to unravel and put them on a chair.

"Might as well do something useful while I'm sitting around," she said, and as the night came, Orville, Ted Olson, and Abe rode off with their lanterns. She pressed her lips to Fargo's as he prepared to leave. "I'm missing you something awful," she said.

"Just a little longer. This thing's going to come to a head soon enough," he told her and, with his lantern, rode into the hills that looked down at Barry's ranch. Once again he watched the lights slowly blink out, those in the main house the last again, and he peered down to the still, silent spread that lay before him. The night wore on and Fargo blinked a number of times to relieve the strain of his eye muscles as he sought the glint of a lantern. None came, but suddenly a light appeared in the bunkhouse to the left, and he made out dark shapes hurrying from the bunkhouse to the stable.

There'd obviously been trouble inside the stable, and Fargo swore silently. This made it unlikely Terence would be signaling. Yet he stayed in place, watching and waiting as the men finally returned from the stable and the bunkhouse light went out again. But the night still had enough hours left in it, and Fargo watched for the lantern. He was frowning when the first pale pink light of dawn touched the distant sky. Of course Terence was down there. He'd know of things there was no way to discern from a distant hilltop, and Fargo turned the Ovaro back toward Orville's place, unhappy at another night of emptiness.

Madge again returned to her place to sleep, and Orville, Abe, and Ted came down from their posts. The day was passed in sleep, and when night came, everyone went off to their places of waiting. Fargo, atop the hill, watched Joe Barry's ranch slowly settle down for the night, the last lights blinking off. As the hours dragged on, there was no unexpected activity below, yet the light he sought did not appear. The moon moved past the midnight sky, and still the ranch remained shrouded in darkness. When the last two nights passed without a signal, he had felt disappointment, but now he was suddenly feeling uneasy. The new day dawn finally tinted the sky, and his uneasiness had become apprehension.

Terence knew the importance of time. Why hadn't he signaled? Were they watching him? If so, why? Had he perhaps asked one question too many? Fargo turned the Ovaro from the hilltop and rode back to Orville's place in the last of the night, apprehension an invisible cloak around him. The others, when they returned, not as tuned-in to possibilities as he, wore disappointment more than apprehension, and Fargo kept his feelings to himself. But when night rolled around again, Fargo woke first, and as the others prepared to take up their positions, he raised a hand.

"Don't ride out, not yet," he said.

"Why not?" Orville asked.

"I want to check out something," Fargo answered.

"Something's gone wrong," Madge said, the alarm instant in her voice.

"I didn't say that," Fargo told her. "Probably not. I just want to have a look for myself. If I'm not back in an hour, then you ride out as usual."

"Whatever you say." Ted Olson nodded and lowered himself into a chair as Madge walked to the Ovaro beside Fargo.

"How will we know that something hasn't happened to you?" she asked.

He returned a wry smile. "If I'm not back come morning," he said. He swung onto the Ovaro and rode away at a fast canter, but this time he didn't send the horse climbing up the low hill to his vantage point. Instead he stayed on the low ground, and before he neared the Barry place he halted, hid the horse in a shadbush thicket, and went on alone. Running through the night in a half crouch, he moved directly toward the front of the ranch, glimpsed two sentries by the main house, and dropped low into a row of rhododendron bushes that paralleled the ranch. They let him move in closer, and he saw that lights were on in the main house and in all the bunkhouses.

He crept closer and watched three men stride across the space between the bunkhouses. His eyes moved through the dim light and came to a halt at the small shack to the side of the stable. He peered at it and the six rifle-bearing guards who surrounded it. He had casually noted the shack when he'd ridden onto the ranch before. There had never been any armed guards near it, and he cursed silently as he knew the meaning of the scene. They were holding somebody inside, and he knew now why there had been no lantern signaling through the night. They had indeed been watching him, and now they had decided to do more than watch him.

Cursing in bitter silence as he backed away and crept through the heavy brush, he knew the full and agonizing impact of the guarded shack. Terence was not simply a prisoner. He was the key to the lives of over forty men. Fargo left the brush, stayed in his crouch, and ran through the darkness to where he had hidden the Ovaro, dropping low to avoid two of Barry's riders who suddenly appeared. He waited and saw two more and then another pair. Barry had sent them out to see if anyone else lay hidden near the ranch. Fargo waited till the men were out of sight, walked the Ovaro from the shadbush, and continued to walk for another five minutes before he swung into the saddle and sent the horse streaking northward. He would barely make it within the hour, he realized.

7

Orville and the others were just preparing to leave when Fargo raced the Ovaro to a halt and leaped to the ground. He saw Madge's eyes fastened on him as he entered the house. "Trouble," he bit out. "Real bad trouble. They have Terence." Madge's gasped half sob broke the silence that followed his words. "You know what that means?" Fargo asked.

"It means that if he talks it's the end of everything," Ted Olson said.

"He won't talk," Madge cut in.

"I'd like to think that, but I can't," Fargo told her gently. "They'll torture him. Damn few men won't talk if they're tortured."

"God. Oh, God," Madge said, turning away, her hands clenched together.

Fargo turned back to the others. "We've got to figure he will. There's no other choice," he said. "When that happens, Joe Barry will know all about our men waiting in the north hills for the signal."

"And he'll send that signal himself," Orville said, a terrible realization in his voice. "He'll send someone out with a lantern and send the signal. Our people will come down; he'll be waiting for them, and it'll be a damn massacre."

"That's right," Fargo said. "Our men are spread

out in the North Hills. We haven't time to get to them. We wouldn't even be able to find them in the dark."

"We'd need a full day to round them up," Abe said.

"There's one chance. If I can get Terence out," Fargo said, his glance scanning the grave faces that watched him, and he paused at Madge. She held her face tight, her hands clenched into fists.

"Can you?" Orville questioned.

"One man might be able to get in. I don't know, but there's a slim chance," Fargo said.

"And if you can't get to him?" Ted Olson asked.

Fargo felt the muscles of his jaw twitch. "I have to see that he doesn't talk, one way or the other," he said flatly and heard Madge's gasp.

"You can't. He did this for you, for all of you," she said.

"I know. I want to get him out. Damn, believe that's what I want," Fargo said. "But if I can't, I've no choice."

"You're talking about my brother's life," Madge flung at him as she fought back tears.

"I'm talking about the lives of forty brothers, husbands, and fathers," he said gently.

Madge hated him at that moment but she understood. It was there, behind the anguish in her eyes, the terrible, heart-rending awareness of the truth in his words. Yet truth, awareness, reality—they were such weak companions in the face of love and loyalty, and she spun away and rushed from the house.

Fargo turned to Orville. "I am going to try to save him," he said and Orville nodded.

"I expect you will," Orville said.

"Anybody have any dynamite sticks?" Fargo said.

"I've got a few, use them for blasting hard rock when I can't dig it," Orville said.

"I'll need two. One I'll use to try to get Terence Noonan out."

"And the other?" Orville asked gravely.

"That'll be in case I can't get him out," Fargo said and hated the saying of it.

"Be right back," Orville said and hurried into the other part of the house. When he returned he was carrying the two sticks of dynamite tied together, and Fargo wedged them securely into his belt. "Good luck," Orville said as Fargo started from the house.

"For all of us," Abe Abelson added, and Fargo started to pull himself onto the Ovaro when he saw the lone, silent figure standing to one side, her back to him. He wanted to reach out, say something reassuring and understanding but realized there were no such words in him. He turned the Ovaro and rode into the darkness, hurrying until he neared the Barry ranch. Once again he hid the Ovaro, but in a thicket of maple closer than the last time. He slid to the ground and moved in a crouch to the front of the ranch and again, he saw two guards at the door of the main house. He skirted behind a line of brush and halted at the edge of a stake-and-picket fence. Beyond it the shack took shape, the six rifle-bearing guards still positioned around it.

He was surveying the land on each side of the shack, gauging the distance to a stand of tall bur oak, when the scream reverberated through the night, a cry of pain rising from inside the shack. Terence's voice died away in a broken sob and then rose again, another agonized scream of pure pain. "Sonofabitch," Fargo murmured aloud. He had no idea how long Terence Noonan had been screaming in pain, but two things were plain, one, he hadn't talked yet, and two, it was damn unlikely he could go on much longer. Fargo's eyes went to the other side of the shack where a dense growth of tall brush ran along the side of the barn. Once again Terence's voice cut into his thoughts, a piercing scream of agony. But this time the scream ended in a string of broken, gasped words. "No . . . no more . . . Jesus, can't take more . . . can't take more," Terence sobbed.

"Damn," Fargo bit out and rose, drawing one of the dynamite sticks from his belt. He lighted the short fuse with a wood match, held it a moment, and then flung it away where it landed between the barn and the line of tall brush. The explosion shattered the night and sent a cloud of wood and tree branches into the air. The guards around the shack whirled and began to run toward the explosion, and Fargo saw the door of the shack open and Joseph and Seth Barry rush out.

They slammed the door behind them as they ran toward where the night had exploded, a cloud of smoke and debris filling the air. "What the hell is it?" he heard Joe Barry shout. Fargo waited thirty seconds and then raced from the picket fence, leaped a hedge, and slammed the door of the shack open. Terence Noonan lay on the ground, all but naked, his body bleeding from wounds in a dozen places. But he was alive, and he started to rise as Fargo stepped in and pulled him to his feet.

"This way," Fargo said and half dragged Terence from the shack. Outside, as he pulled the younger man across the ground, he heard the shouts of Barry and his men as they milled around the site of the explosion. He had almost reached the line of bur oak when the two shots rang out, both whizzing past his head. He dropped and rolled as another pair of shots exploded. Out of the corner of his eye he saw Terence collapse on the ground, but there were more shots now, other riflemen running toward him. "Shit," he swore as he dived into the trees with no chance to take Terence with him. He had but seconds to save his own neck as a volley of shots came through the darkness.

Staying crouched, Fargo ran through the bur oak and heard Joe Barry's voice barking commands. "Get this bastard back into the shack," Barry ordered. "Then take ten men and search every damn inch around here." Fargo continued to run and heard the sound of footsteps racing in different directions behind him. They were circling, spreading out, and he dropped low in the trees, groped inside their blackness, and almost stumbled upon two fallen logs, all but invisible in the dark. He wedged himself between the logs and listened to the searchers rush back and forth all around him.

Finally they broke off their searching, and he heard them return to the Barry ranch. He rose and retraced steps through the oak until he was again across from the shack. He saw the door open and Barry and his son emerge. "We'll get back to him in a few minutes. I want to see how much the barn is damaged," Barry said, and he paused to sweep the six rifle-toting guards with a harsh glance. "Anybody but Seth or me comes near the shack you shoot, understand?" he snapped.

"Yes, sir," the men answered almost in unison,

and Barry strode away, Seth at his heels. Fargo waited, let the guards settle down around the shack, and then he pulled the last stick of dynamite from his belt. He'd never be able to get near the shack again, he knew. The attempt to rescue Terence had failed and he'd not get another. As for Terence, he was about to crack. He'd certainly do so at the next round of torture. Fargo thought again of the bitterness of his task. Madge's proud, fine face came into his thoughts and then the grave faces of all the men who wanted to save their lands.

He swore silently as he lighted the fuse, held it for another moment, and then flung the dynamite in a high arc through the night. He saw it crash against the door of the shack, and the nearest men whirled in surprise, frozen for a moment. It exploded as they were staring at it, sending the shack flying upward in a cascade of wood. Fargo saw three of the men sent sailing into the air. One landed against the picket fence, impaled on one of the pickets, and the other two hurtled into a tree with such force the imprint of their flattened, bloodied faces marked the trunk.

Over the din and the shouting Fargo heard Joseph Barry's voice in rage as Fargo raced back through the bur oak to the Ovaro. He climbed into the saddle and sent the horse galloping away, down the road and then north to Moon Lake. It was over, that much of it, and he knew bitterness would ride with him for too long. Orville opened the door as he reached his place and slid to the ground. Inside the room Madge waited with the others, standing, and he saw her eyes search his face. He knew she read the answers there, but he had to give something, a kind of apology. "I tried. I almost pulled it off," he said.

He saw her lips tremble as she slowly walked from the house, and he turned to Orville, Abe, and Ted. "We know the rest, just as she does," Orville said. Fargo let himself sink into one of the straight-backed chairs.

"The Barrys know something. They know Terence was stopped from talking because there was a plan," Fargo said.

"But they don't know what," Ted said.

"No, they don't, but they know they can't wait around. This'll trigger them into moving on you," Fargo said. "Tomorrow night, I'd guess."

"That'll give us all day to find the others in the hills and bring them down," Orville said.

"Find them, tell them what happened, but keep them in the hills," Fargo said, and the three men stared back at him.

"Keep them up there?" Abe echoed.

"Bring them down and you'll be having the pitched battle Barry wants and what we've been trying to avoid," Fargo said. "Let him attack. Let him burn down your houses if that's what he wants. Houses can be rebuilt and replaced. Lives can't. He figures to wipe you out so you won't own the land anymore. You won't have squatters rights to any of it. You'll be dead, most of you. I want him to carry out his attack, and when he's finished he'll realize he hasn't won a thing. You'll all still be alive somewhere, all still owning your land."

"Then he'll come searching for us," Abe said.

"It'll take him awhile to regroup for that," Fargo said. "Meanwhile, I'm going to find a way into his house. I'm going to learn what this is all about.

When I have that, we'll arrange a second chance to turn the tables on Barry."

"Meanwhile, we just go and join the others," Orville said.

"Unless you want to stay here and let Barry's men kill you," Fargo said.

"What about Madge. She's gone home by now," Orville mentioned.

"I'll bring Madge to the North Hills tomorrow," Fargo said.

"We'll be watching for you," Ted called after him as he walked from the house and rode into the night. He circled the silent lake until he reached Madge's place and saw the lamplight still on. He halted and dismounted as she opened the door.

"I wondered if you'd dare to come by," she said.

"You can stop wondering," he said, stepping inside.

"Get out," she said, and he saw the wetness still on her cheeks. "You killed my brother, damn you." He saw her hand come up and made no move to block it. The slap stung his cheek, and then she was against him, sobbing into his chest, her arms encircling him. "Damn you, damn you," she murmured between sobs and he held her until she stopped and stepped back.

"I only came by to tell you I'm taking you into the North Hills tomorrow. You'll stay there with everyone else until it's time to come down," Fargo said. "Get together whatever you need to take with you."

"Why into the North Hills?" she asked, and he quickly told her of the decisions that had been made. She turned from him and began to stuff blouses and slips into a canvas sack, and when she finished she turned back to him. "You'll come back for me come morning?" she asked, and he nodded and started for the door when he felt her hand on his arm. "There's no need for that. Stay the night," she said. "With me, holding me."

"You surprise me," he said.

"Yes, I'm sure I do. But I thought about all of this after I left you at Orville's. I couldn't go to bed with the man who killed my brother, but I know I can't see you as that. I see you only as the man who saved the lives of dozens and dozens of men."

"I'm glad," he said as she led him into her room, and it was but moments later that she was lying with him, her smoothness pressed against him.

"Make me forget, Fargo. Make me forget everything," Madge murmured.

"It won't last," he told her.

"I don't care. I'll settle for a little forgetting," she said, and he felt her tufted nap rubbing against him, and the slender thighs opened and came around him. Suddenly she was afire, a new, desperate wildness to her that refused to be denied. She made love to him with every part of her body, sweeping him along with the sheer intensity of her steel-wire inner tensions, and her climax was a thing of screaming pleasure that somehow seemed to hold all the despair in the world in it. Finally she slept beside him, but her sleep was made of sudden twitchings, little cries that escaped her lips without her waking. When morning came she woke as he rose. Fargo finished washing and was dressed when she came into the kitchen.

She had put on a simple dark green shirt and riding britches and there was a beautiful sadness in her face. "I'm ready," she said simply and left the room with her sack. She had her mare saddled when he went outside and climbed onto the pinto, and she rode in silence beside him as he made his way up into the densely forested North Hills with their thick stands of quaking aspen and white fir. He halted as he glimpsed the six horsemen appear and recognized Orville and Lem Carter as they drew closer.

"We'll take her now, Fargo," Orville said and Madge looked surprised as she turned to the big man beside her.

"You're not staying?" she asked.

"I want to make sure when Barry attacks," Fargo said. "I'll be back." He turned the horse in a small circle and rode away as Madge went with Orville and the others. Fargo rode carefully out of the North Hills, scanning the terrain before moving into the open. He rode back toward Moon Lake with his eyes sweeping the land for any sight of Barry's men, and he finally drew to a halt and moved into a heavy stretch of box elder across from Orville's place. If he came directly from his place, Joseph Barry would reach Orville's place first at the bottom end of the circular lake.

Fargo moved up onto a low hill that held a heavy stretch of good thick hackberry and let himself and the Ovaro disappear into the trees. He hadn't long to wait when he saw the dark mass of riders galloping toward Orville's house. Barry had decided not to split his men up but to attack each place with his full force, Fargo noted, and he watched them move on Orville's place, laying down a heavy barrage of rifle fire first. Then a dozen men on foot rushed the house followed by another dozen. Fargo glimpsed Joseph Barry to one side, and he saw Seth leading the second wave of attacks.

Seth emerged in moments. "There's nobody here," he called to his father. "Not a goddamn person."

"Maybe they're going to make a stand at one of the other places. Let's go," Joe Barry called, and Fargo watched the large group of horsemen start off to the right. They'd reach John Otis's place next, Fargo knew as he backed from the trees and sent the Ovaro racing westward. They'd be a good hour at least going from place to place, maybe two; he smiled as he rode through the night. He neared Barry's ranch and rode as close as he dared before dismounting and hurrying forward on foot to halt behind a bush that faced the front of the main house.

As he'd expected, Barry had taken almost everyone with him, leaving only two guards. Fargo crept along the bush and darted through an open space to a longer line of rhodedendron. One guard stood watch at one corner of the house, the other some fifty feet away. Fargo circled, staying in a crouch. Neither of the men were on alert, each casually leaning against a corner post of the house. Though he held the Colt in his hand, Fargo didn't want to use it. These were probably the only two Barry had left behind, but he couldn't be certain.

He waited, watched the nearest guard, and when the man yawned and bent his head down to light a cigarette, Fargo streaked from the bushes to the side of the house where he instantly dropped to one knee. Directly behind the guard now, he started to move forward, sliding one step at a time. But the man's back stayed to him as he continued to puff on his cigarette. Fargo said silent thanks that the guard was neither alert nor intuitive as he reached the man, brought the butt of the Colt down hard on the back of the man's head, and caught the figure before it fell.

He lowered the guard to the ground, let him stay propped up against the base of the column, and flattened himself on the ground behind him. It took perhaps another five minutes for the other guard to notice him. "Willie? What're you doin'?" the second guard called. "Get up, you don't want Barry catching you like that." But as Willie didn't move, the second guard's voice took on alarm. "Willie? What's the matter? You sick or somethin'?" he called. But the seated figure remained silent and motionless, and Fargo heard the second man hurrying to him. The guard halted, dropped to one knee, and bent over to lift up his partner's face. Fargo seized the moment, half rose, and slammed the Colt across the second guard's temple. The man pitched forward on top of the first one and lay still.

Fargo straightened up and was at the door of the house in three strides. He pulled it open, saw that lamps were on to light the hallways and most of the rooms, and he remembered Terence had said the safe was in a study. He hurried down a wide corridor and came to a square room, wood-paneled with a large desk and three leather easy chairs. He spotted the safe against the far wall at once and dropped to his knee beside it. It was far thicker and heavier than he'd expected. Even a bullet from the powerful Colt wouldn't shatter the steel, and he put his ear down to the lock as he began to carefully turn the cylinder. He worked on it for some fifteen minutes and realized he was wasting his time. He was no safe-cracker and the combination lock was not simple. He should've brought one of Orville's dynamite sticks, he realized, and he got to his feet.

He'd have to return, find a way to draw Barry away, and return with the dynamite, he muttered silently. Meanwhile, he'd try to make it a little easier next time. There had to be a storm door into the cellar someplace, and he hurried from the room and made his way down the corridor, opening doors as he went along. He found a coat closet and two broom closets before he came onto a door with steps behind it leading downward. He started down and saw the glow of a lamp in the cellar. He was halfway down the stairs when the voice came to him.

"Water. I need water, dammit," the voice said, a high-pitched, quavering tone. Fargo continued down, and surprise swept through him as he saw a cell taking up most of the cellar, iron bars from floor to ceiling. An old man looked up at him from inside the cell. He was wearing only trousers, the rest of his frail body shirtless and shoeless. His face, smudged with dirt, comprised sunken cheeks, watery blue eyes, and long, gray, stringy hair. "Don't hit me. I'm thirsty. I need water," the old man said and took up a tin bowl and gestured to a keg alongside the wall.

"I'm not going to hit you," Fargo said, and the old man pushed the tin bowl through the bars at him. Fargo took it and dipped it into the water inside the keg and slipped the bowl through a small opening at the bottom of the bars. "Who are you?" he asked as the old man drank thirstily.

"Enoch. Enoch Bender," the man said between gulps.

Fargo paused, a hundred questions for the old man pushing at him, but first things first. He'd come into the cellar to prepare something vital, and he stepped past the cell, his eyes scanning the dimness, and then he spied it, an oblong storm cellar door near one wall. He reached it in four strides and saw the dead bolt that held it locked. He slid the bolt back, and the door appeared exactly as it was unless it came under close inspection. But the bolt was unlocked, the horizontal door ready to be opened from outside.

He turned back to the old man, who had halted his thirsty gulping. "Why are you locked up here, Enoch Bender?" Fargo asked.

The frail figure gave a shrug. "Joe Barry," Enoch said.

"You did something to Joe Barry?" Fargo questioned.

"Didn't do anythin' to him. Did the mean bastard a real favor," the old man said.

"Then why are you locked in a cell down here?" Fargo pressed.

"Because he's a damn liar. Because he's no good," Enoch Bender said.

"How long have you been held down here?" Fargo asked.

The old man screwed up his face as he thought and peered upward at the ceiling. "Can't say. Lost track of time down here," he said.

"Take a guess," Fargo said.

" 'Bout a year," Enoch Bender said, and Fargo was about to question him further when he heard the sounds of hoofbeats and horses riding to a halt.

"Damn," he muttered and spun. There was no time to question the old man further. Swearing silently, he bolted up the stairs. They were back sooner than he'd expected, but he realized there was something to be grateful for in that. It meant they hadn't taken the time to torch houses. He reached the top of the stairs and pushed into the corridor just as footsteps echoed outside the door. He paused and realized he'd no time to reach a window and nowhere to go if he did with a horde of Barry's men still milling around outside.

He dived into one of the broom closets and pulled the door shut as Joe Barry and Seth stormed into the house. "I've got everybody searching the ranch grounds, Pa," Fargo heard Seth say.

"Go down and check on the old geezer," Joe Barry growled. They had found the two guards, Fargo grunted silently. He listened to Seth Barry clatter down the stairs while the senior Barry strode into the living room and then the study. Fargo crouched silently inside the closet as Seth returned.

"He's down there," Seth Barry called to his father.

"Nothing wrong in here," the elder Barry said. "But he was in here, goddamn him, I know it."

"Fargo?" Seth Barry said.

"Who the hell else?" Joe Barry snarled. "He's back of all of it. Those dumbheads wouldn't be able to pull this off. He's got them hiding someplace so we wouldn't wipe them out. But it won't work. We'll comb every goddamn inch of this territory until we find them. We'll let the men rest a day, and then we'll start searching for the bastards."

"Maybe they just hightailed it," Fargo heard Seth offer.

"And leave their land for me? Shit, they wouldn't be that dumb," Barry said. "No, they might be, but

Fargo wouldn't let them. Doesn't matter. We'll track them down. Let's get some goddamn sleep."

Fargo remained crouched in the dark of the closet and listened to the Barrys go their ways into adjoining rooms, doors slammed behind them. Fargo stayed listening and heard the searchers outside returning, stabling their horses, and finally the ranch settling down to stillness. Fargo forced himself to wait another half hour before he crept from the closet, moving on the balls of his feet. He edged the front door open and peered out the crack. There were no guards posted. Weariness and conceit always made for mistakes, Fargo commented silently as he streaked across the ground, past the stables and out of the ranch to where he had left the Ovaro. He walked the horse for a hundred yards before climbing into the saddle and riding north toward Moon Lake.

There were not many hours left in the night when he reached the lake and he decided to bed down and gather some sleep. Beneath the low branches of a bur oak he slept through the first sun, the body demanding payment, and he finally woke, washed, ate from a raspberry bush, and then rode into the North Hills. Orville, Lem Carter, and Madge were the trio that came to meet him, and he halted to face the apprehension in their faces. "We did well. Nobody's home was burned down," he told them, and the relief swam into their eyes. "Anybody ever hear of a man named Enoch Bender?" he asked.

They shook heads almost as one. "Never heard anybody mention that name," Orville said. "Why?"

"Barry's holding him prisoner in a cell in his cellar," Fargo said. "An old man, half-crazy maybe, yet aware enough to call Joe Barry names."

"Why is he there?" Madge asked.

"That's what I'd like knowing," Fargo said. "Somehow, I think it's tied up with why Barry is after your lands. Just a guess, but I feel it inside. I'm going back into Barry's place tonight."

"That's suicide," Madge cut in.

"I left myself a way in," Fargo said.

"It's still suicide," Madge said.

"Barry intends to take his men and comb the land until he finds you," Fargo said. "Sooner or later he'll be coming up here into the North Hills."

"We'll round the others up, wait for him, and give him a damn greeting he'll never forget," Lem Carter said.

"That's a nice plan that won't work," Fargo said.

"Why not? We've some forty men." Lem Carter frowned.

"He's got some sixty. You're plenty outgunned. You'd need a real surprise to even the odds," Fargo said. "But that's not why it won't work. Think it through some more. Put yourself in Barry's shoes." He waited and watched Orville, Lem, and Madge frown in thought.

"I can't figure why it won't work," Lem said.

"Barry finally starts combing these hills and you're waiting for him. You've everyone together and dug in, and you start firing as he comes in," Fargo outlined. "What's he do? He falls back right away, and now he knows where you are. He has the strength to surround you. That's all he has to do for starters, surround you and wait."

Orville's frown grew darker. "Surround us and keep us pinned down," he murmured.

"You're all just about out of provisions now. You'll be needing food and water. Sooner or later you're going to have to come down and try to break through. He'll be waiting for that with all the advantages of cover, firepower, and angle. You'll have given him the classic position, and he'll massacre you."

"Goddamn," Orville muttered, but Fargo heard the realization in his voice.

"You came up here and spread out so's you could be safe until it was time to attack at that signal that never came. Then you stayed to avoid his full attack. You stay and wait for him, and you'll turn this place into a trap for yourselves," Fargo said.

"You saying we go back to our places?" Orville asked.

"No. I'm saying we spring the trap. We choose the time and place," Fargo said.

"Go on. We're listening," Lem Carter said.

"I'll spell it all out for you and leave it to you to tell the others," Fargo said. "If I can do my part, you just be ready and waiting." His eyes met Madge's for a moment as Orville and Lem settled down to listen. He wanted to send silent reassurance to her and found the best he could do was offer a gambler's chance.

8

Surrounded by the night, Fargo peered down at the Barry ranch and knew that, dead or alive, this would be his last visit. The strange chain of events had begun with deception and death. Would it end the same way? He allowed a grim smile to edge his lips. There was more than a passing likelihood. The course of action had been set for everyone, perhaps himself most of all. If things went according to plan, poor Ben Adams and Ellie Willis would not have died in vain. *If*. He grunted and let the word hang in front of him as he dismounted and settled down against the bark of an old, thick mountain ash, its flattened white flowers a soft pattern over his head.

He let himself doze in the deep silence of the night. Timing was crucial. He needed the cover of darkness, but he also needed the new day hanging on the horizon and ready to rise. He needed to be unseen and he needed to be seen. The contradictions had a rhyme and a reason, if he could use them both. When he woke from his third doze, he rose and saw the moon just beginning to dip down over the distant hills. The time was at hand. He turned the Ovaro and started down toward the Barry ranch, once more hiding the horse in a dense thicket facing the rear of the main house this time.

He slid to the ground and began to crawl on his stomach toward the house.

Barry had his guards all placed at the front of the house, and Fargo made his way toward the rear where the storm cellar door lay flat against the ground. He reached it, drew up to one knee, and carefully lifted the wide, flat door and held it open just wide enough for himself to slip into the house. He eased the door down into place again from the top step and saw the glow from below. They apparently kept the kerosense lamp on all night beside the cell. He silently went down the few steps to the cell with Enoch Bender inside. The old man was sitting up on the mattress on the floor, and he pushed to his feet as Fargo came into view.

"Who are you?" The old man asked, peering at Fargo as he came close to the cell.

"I was here yesterday, Enoch. Remember?" Fargo said.

The old man frowned at him and was obviously having difficulty marshaling memory. "You a friend of Joe Barry?" he asked.

"Not exactly," Fargo whispered. "Now you stay real quiet and maybe I can come back and get you out of there." He began to cross to the stairs and saw the old man watching him with a strangely quizzical expression. He pressed one finger to his lips as he began to climb the stairs. Enoch Bender was still peering up at him as he reached the top, and Fargo slowly pushed the door open and stepped into the dim corridor, a hurricane lamp at the far end. On the balls of his feet he proceeded down the corridor to halt at one closed door. He listened, heard a cough and the sound of someone turning over in bed. Carefully he inched the door open enough to see into the room. The last of the moonlight filtered in through a window, just enough for him to see Seth Barry's face and shoulders over the bedsheet. He quietly closed the door and hurried down the corridor to the other end where another closed door waited.

He put his ear to it and caught short, spasmodic snoring sounds, and he edged the door open and stepped into what was plainly the master bedroom, spacious with a large bed in the center. Wearing only the bottoms of his longjohns, Joe Barry lay on the bed atop the sheet. Fargo unholstered the Colt as he crossed the room silently as a panther to halt at the side of the bed. He pressed the barrel of the Colt against Joe Barry's cheekbone, and the man woke instantly, his eyes popping open. "Getting-up time," Fargo said softly.

He kept the revolver against the man's cheekbone as Joe Barry sat up, blinking at the figure in front of him. "You," Barry breathed. "You must be a real crazy man."

"Maybe," Fargo said. "But you're going to be a real dead man unless you do exactly what I say." He kept the gun against Joe Barry's face as the man swung his legs from the bed.

"Can I put my damn pants on?" Barry muttered as he reached for trousers hanging over a nearby chair. Fargo stepped back and let the man pull on trousers as he kept the Colt trained on him. Barry turned to him, a frown of disbelief furrowing his brow. "You'll never get out of here alive," the man growled.

"If I don't, you don't," Fargo said with a quick glance at the window. The last of the night still clung, and he motioned with the Colt. "Into the study," he said. "You first." The man glared but turned as the Colt jammed into his back. He led the way from the room to the next doorway and entered. Fargo glimpsed a kerosense lamp on a table. "Turn it on," he ordered and kept the Colt into Barry's back as the man obeyed and the lamp spread light into the room. He marched Barry to the safe and pressed him down on one knee. "Open it," he said. Barry half turned and shot him a glance of rage, and Fargo put the Colt to the back of his head. "Don't stall for time. You haven't got any and I'm very nervous," he said.

Joseph Barry began to twist the dial of the combination lock while Fargo kept the revolver against him. He turned it to the right, then right again, back to the left and Fargo pulled the hammer back on the Colt. The click sounded loud as a cannon shot in the room and Fargo saw Joseph Barry go pale. He turned the dial once more and the safe came open. Fargo drew the Colt back and let the hammer down. "Empty it," he ordered, and Barry reached into the safe and pulled out two bags of coins and a bound sheaf of bills. "The rest. Hurry up," Fargo demanded, and Barry removed a ledger book. Fargo flung him to the floor as he cursed, reached into the safe, and pulled out a crinkled piece of parchment. He kept the gun on Barry as the man sat up, and Fargo spread the square of parchment on the wood floorboards. Flicking his eyes from Barry to the parchment, back and forth, he took in the drawings on the square in quick glances; they took shape and became an outline of Moon Lake.

He saw markings around the edges of the lines that marked the shore, others extending into what appeared to be the lake itself. In another quick glance he saw a weaving network of lines that ran through Madge's property, Orville's, Lem Carter's, and everyone else's that bordered Moon Lake. The markings began to suddenly take on meaning, their own crude but unquestionable meaning. "These are gold veins," he said, and Barry's glowering silence was an admission. "This map says there's gold in the land around Moon Lake and under the lake itself," Fargo said and heard the surprise in his voice turning to sudden comprehension. "That's why you wanted to get rid of everybody with land along the lake. That's why you tried buying them out and then, when they wouldn't sell, decided to force them out."

"You'll never live to tell anybody, Fargo," Barry said.

Fargo cast a glance at the window. There was still darkness on the land. "That's what Ben Adams found out, and you had him murdered and made it look like an accident," he said. "Then you couldn't be sure he hadn't told Ellie Willis, so you had her poisoned. Somehow you found out she'd written to me."

"She talked too much," Barry said.

"So you had to try and stop me from getting here in time to talk to Ellie," Fargo said, and once again Barry's tight-lipped glower was his answer. Fargo touched the parchment with one finger. "This explains that old man in the cell. Enoch Bender's an old prospector. He discovered these gold veins. He made this map," Fargo said. "Somehow, you got hold of it, but I don't understand why you've kept him alive."

The voice that answered was not Joseph Barry's.

"We figured we might need him when we started mining," it said. "Now drop the damn gun." Fargo swore under his breath and let the Colt slide from his fingers. It landed on the floor, and the sound had a ring of death in it. He turned to see Seth Barry with a big Remington–Beals Navy revolver in hand, a fast-shooting, single-action, six-shot weapon. Seth Barry wore a satisfied smirk on his face as he came into the room, and his father scooped up Fargo's Colt. "Too bad you didn't know, Fargo," the younger man said.

"Know what?" Fargo queried.

"That the first thing I do when I wake is to go down and check on old Enoch," Seth Barry said.

"He told you I was up here?"

"That's right. The old fool's always trying to make a deal. He said he had a secret he'd tell me if I promised to let him out," Seth said. "He got real cute, refused to say anything until I let him out. So I let him out and he told me about you. I threw him back in again soon as he finished." He turned to his father. "You want to shoot him, Pa?"

"Not so fast. We have a bargaining chip here that'll bring in all his pals," the elder Barry said. "We send out a couple of the boys and get out word that we have him and we'll bargain for him."

"You think they'll do that?" Seth questioned.

"Of course they will. We draw them in, make promises and demands and then be ready to take out the whole lot of them," Joseph Barry said and almost chuckled at the thought. "It may take a few days but they'll come."

"And him?" Seth gestured.

"We keep him alive, in case we have to show

him," Joseph Barry said. "Take him downstairs and lock him in the cell with the old fool."

"Move," Seth growled, and Fargo walked to the door of the room and felt Seth Barry poke the Remington into his back. "Downstairs. You know the way," Seth said with a mocking laugh, and Fargo reached the stairs to the cellar and started down. He swore silently, aware that the big Remington fired too quickly for him to try to bolt. The dawn was pushing away the last of the night, he knew. Time was running out for him. "Put your hands on the bars," Seth ordered and Fargo closed his fingers around the iron uprights as Seth unlocked the cell door, held it open, and Fargo walked into the cell.

He turned as Seth slammed the door shut and went up the stairs. He was alone with Enoch Bender. He wanted to call the old prospector a fool, but the words stuck inside him as he saw Enoch's watery eyes stare at him. "Seth's no friend of yours, Enoch. You shouldn't have told him," Fargo said without reproach.

"He said he was my friend," Enoch said.

"You told me Joe Barry was a no-good bastard," Fargo said.

The old prospector thought for a moment and then his gray eyebrows lowered. "Yes, he is and I said that. That's right and so's Seth," Enoch agreed.

Fargo grimaced. It was plain that the old man's mind had fits of wandering and moments of lucidness. It was also plain he could be triggered into either. "When you discovered the gold around and under Moon Lake, why didn't you stake your claims to the land then?" Fargo asked.

"I'd another vein I'd found out near the Oregon Territory. I decided to work that one first and then come back to Moon Lake. Guess you could say I saw Moon Lake as a bird-in-the-hand I could pick up whenever I was ready. Hell, it was all open land then."

"What happened?" Fargo pressed.

"Fell down a mine shaft by my other vein. Couldn't even walk for five years, didn't even know where I was. It was ten years before I got better and found my Oregon Territory vein wasn't any good. I came back to Moon Lake to find all the land owned. I met the Barrys and told them I'd a business proposition for them. If they could get my land free, I'd go halves with them on the gold."

"Instead they took your map, slammed you into the jail, and they held all the cards," Fargo said and the old prospector nodded his head slowly.

"They told me I could trust them," Enoch said.

Fargo turned from the old man and reached down to the calf-holster under his trousers that held the thin, razor-sharp, double-edged throwing knife. The cell lock was an old-style, simple device, and Fargo began to probe into it with the point of the narrow blade. He felt the tumbler pin and carefully worked the blade tip along the smooth side until he found the head. He pressed, heard the tumbler begin to give, and then the blade slipped away and he swore silently as he began again. This time he managed to keep the tip of the knife in place, and the tumbler moved back as he heard the click of the lock opening. He pushed the door open at once and stepped from the cell, crossed to the stairs in three bounding strides, and glanced back as he climbed the steps. Enoch Bender was still in the cell, staring at the open door with a strange indecision, suddenly free on his own and paralyzed by the very reality of it.

Fargo reached the top of the stairs and edged himself through the doorway. He heard sounds down the corridor as the ranch began to waken and Seth Barry's voice echoed from a distant room. Fargo ran in a long, silent lope and reached the open door of the study just as Joe Barry was putting the square of parchment back into the safe. The Colt lay on the desk, Fargo saw as he crossed the room. Joe Barry felt someone's presence and spun around just as Fargo's fist crashed into his jaw. The man flew backward, struck the safe, and slid to the floor. "Shit," Fargo cursed as he saw the safe door began to swing closed. He kicked out and got his foot in between the door and the edge of the safe just in time to keep the door from slamming shut.

He reached into the safe, yanked the piece of parchment out, folded it and stuffed it into his pocket. Joe Barry was shaking his head, starting to focus as Fargo scooped the Colt from the desktop and ran for the door. Behind him Joe Barry's voice rose. "Goddamn, stop that bastard. Seth, get in here," the man screamed as Fargo raced into the corridor and headed for the rear of the house. He looked back without slowing his racing legs to see Seth Barry appear at the other end of the house.

"Jesus," he heard Seth shout and saw the man draw his gun. But Fargo reached the window as the first shot slammed into the wall, and he dived headlong through the open bottom, his legs scraping the sill. He hit the ground rolling, and behind he heard Joe Barry and Seth shouting commands and racing to the front door. Fargo allowed a grim smile as he streaked across the ground in the new morning sun. It could still work, he realized, and Joe Barry's voice split the morning air.

"Get everybody," the man shouted. "Everybody hit the saddle."

Fargo heard the confusion of shouts and running feet, the stable doors being flung open and horses pulled out. The sounds grew dimmer as he plunged through the brush to where the Ovaro had been hidden. He untied the reins and climbed into the saddle and sent the horse moving out onto an open stretch of hillside in plain view of those at the ranch.

"There he is, goddammit. Get him," Fargo heard Joe Barry shout, and he glanced back to see Seth Barry starting toward the hillside, his entire force of hired gunslingers following. Fargo stayed in the open, turned, darted through a line of shadbush, and emerged into the open again. He glanced back and saw the pursuers swerve to go after him, and now Joe Barry was in the lead.

Fargo turned the Ovaro west and continued to dodge in and out of tree cover, making sure that Barry and his men could always catch sight of him. As he neared a long ridge, he saw Seth Barry take half the men and split away to ride along one side of the ridge while his father took his force along the other side. Fargo stayed on the ridge, aware that the two pursuing forces were gaining on him. He kept the Ovaro at its pace, let Barry's men come almost abreast of him, and then let the Ovaro surge forward. The ridge turned downward, and he saw both of his pursuing bands start to move in on him to sandwich him in between. He didn't fear that. The Ovaro had plenty of power in him to rocket away, but suddenly Fargo's eyes opened and the curse stuck in his throat.

The ridge didn't go downward onto flat land. It halted at the edge of a wide chasm, undoubtedly the result of rainwater over the years. The flat land beckoned beyond, but there was no horse, including the Ovaro, that could leap the chasm that loomed larger as he neared the edge. He reined the horse to a halt and saw Seth Barry turning his men to come at him from one side, the elder Barry doing the same from the other side. But they weren't shooting. Joe Barry still wanted him alive as bait. Fargo stayed in place, his eyes measuring distances as the two groups of pursuers raced at him. They were almost at the top of the ridge when he spun the pinto and raced back the way he'd come, cutting clean through both sets of riders. To be safe, he stayed flattened across the pinto's neck as he ran the gauntlet, and when he glanced back he saw both Joe Barry's men and Seth's almost collide on top of the ridge.

They had to fall away in confusion as there were too many to ride along the ridgetop, and Fargo had already put a dozen yards between himself and them. They returned down to the sides of the ridge when Fargo suddenly cut to the right and raced downward almost in front of Seth Barry's nose. He continued on, found a clear space, and galloped across it as Seth turned his men to follow. Fargo crossed a small stream and glanced back to see Joe Barry had come up alongside Seth, the others back to one group now. Fargo made a wide circle across the terrain as the others charged behind him. They continued to follow as he entered a terrain of thickly grown tree cover, mostly white fir and cottonwood, with enough open land to allow him to keep up speed. The others fell back a little when they had to spread out to avoid running into trees.

He eased up the Ovaro slightly so they wouldn't lose sight of him, and when he saw the broad stretch of panic grass he sent the horse charging across it. It was the first mark he sought, and then he spied the second, a tall line of Douglas fir, and halfway across the broad stretch he spotted the third one, a deep cut in between thickly foliaged terrain. He reined to a halt, let the Ovaro draw in a handful of deep breaths, and cast a look of fright back at the horde of riders that raced at him. As if in panic, he spun the pinto in a half circle and headed for the deep cut, plunging into it at full speed. Another quick glance behind showed Seth Barry in the lead as the others charged into the cut after him.

He galloped on, the cut long as well as deep, and he saw that his pursuers were all inside the cut, unable to ride more then four abreast. The tiny furrow was just edging across his brow when the cut erupted in a cascade of gunfire, and Fargo reined to a halt, spun the pinto around, and saw almost a third of Barry's men go down with the first burst of shots that came from both sides of the cut. "Go get them, goddammit," he heard Seth Barry shout above the gunfire, and he saw the man start to lead one portion of his men into the trees at the right while the elder Barry took his forces into the trees at the other side. Another strong volley of shots exploded, and Fargo saw them take their toll of Barry's men.

But the battle was inside the thick tree cover now, and Fargo sent the Ovaro into the trees as he drew the Colt, took a bead on one of Barry's men, and fired. The rider toppled from his horse to lay still in a clump of pigweed. Fargo glimpsed Orville firing at three horsemen who raced on both sides of him, his shots missing all three. Sending the Ovaro forward, Fargo dropped from the saddle to land almost beside Orville, hunker down, and fire off two shots at two of the riders who circled back. The first one fell forward across his saddle, hung there for a moment, and then slid to the ground as his horse stopped. The second one clutched at his side suddenly pouring crimson, tried to hang onto his reins, and finally tumbled out of the saddle.

"It worked, goddamn, it worked, Fargo," Orville said as he reloaded and Fargo did the same. "I was getting worried about you."

"Unexpected delays," Fargo said and ducked low as two shots whizzed over his head. The shooter raced into the foliage before he could return fire, and Fargo listened to the gunfire that erupted all around him and from the other side of the cut. There was no way to determine how well the ranchers were doing, but Barry had lost heavily in the first volleys. Yet he had surprised him, Fargo realized. He'd expected the man to turn and race his forces out of the cut, but Barry had mounted a counterattack.

Fargo saw the swift-moving shapes of four riders fleeing through the trees. They were clearly running, and Fargo leaped onto the Ovaro as the gunfire on this side of the cut began to subside. He raced after the four riders and saw them burst into the open land of the cut, turn, and start to race away. As he watched, three shots rang out and one of the fleeing riders went down, but the other three were almost out of range. The gunfire from the trees on the other side continued, and Fargo started to race across the cut when a shot grazed his arm and he swerved the pinto as the second shot went wide of its mark. He turned to see Seth Barry racing at him, firing as he did, and Fargo dropped low as another bullet hurtled just past his head. He brought his own gun up and fired, but Seth Barry had swerved his horse in anticipation and Fargo's shot missed.

The man yanked his mount to a halt and leaped to the ground. Firing from behind his horse, he sent two more bullets winging, and Fargo had to slide down along the Ovaro's side to avoid the shots. He clung there for a moment, then let himself drop to the ground. He struck the grass and rolled, came up on his stomach in line with Seth Barry, and fired two shots. He saw one graze Barry's hip, and the man spin around as the second shot caught his leg. Seth Barry fell to one knee as he fired furiously, emptying his gun, and Fargo had to roll again to avoid being caught by one of the shots.

When he came up on his stomach again, he saw Seth Barry racing at him on foot, drawing a second gun from inside his shirt, a Remington pocket pistol. His lips drawn back in rage, Seth Barry let fury destroy aim, and his shots were once again a wild fusillade. But a wild bullet could kill as surely as an aimed one, Fargo knew, and he rolled again, this time into a clump of brush. Still firing, Seth Barry veered toward the brush, and Fargo took aim and fired two shots, the second one following the first one's trajectory without a fraction of an inch's difference. Seth Barry halted in his tracks as if he'd smashed into an invisible wall. He shuddered and quivered, and the middle of his chest had suddenly become a red fountain. He sank down on both knees, swayed there for a moment and then pitched forward onto his face.

Fargo rose and realized the gunfire had ended, and he saw a half dozen figures rising from the ground. He made out Lem Carter and Alton Harris and the two men came toward him. "It's over. We did it. You did it," Lem Carter said.

"You were right the first time. We," Fargo said. "He took me by surprise by charging. How many did you lose?"

"Don't know yet. We'll take a count after we see who walks into the cut," Lem said.

Fargo nodded and the two men walked on, and then he spotted the glint of dark-blond hair emerging from behind a tree. "They brought everybody," he said as Madge came up to him.

"I insisted. My land, my fight. Most of the women decided to come and fight beside their husbands," she said. She stood beside him as he watched the shadowy shapes moving slowly down through the trees toward the open cut. He made a quick count that he knew was inaccurate, yet he counted enough to know that they had done well. He felt Madge's body lean against his. "I kept wondering if you were going to show or if something else had gone wrong," she said.

"Almost," he admitted. "Let's go down to the others." She nodded and started to walk through the trees with him when the voice came, very soft yet very recognizable.

"I got a bead right on her head " it said. "Don't move or she gets it." Fargo halted and felt Madge freeze beside him, and then Joseph Barry came into sight, a big Walker in his hands, the rifle leveled at Madge's head. "Drop your gun, Fargo," the man said. Fargo, his lips a thin line, let the Colt fall to the ground. "Kick it away," Barry ordered, and Fargo sent the gun skittering through the grass. "You, too, girlie," Barry ordered, and Madge let her rifle fall to the ground. The man stepped a pace closer, the rifle still held at Madge when with a quick, sudden movement, he swung the heavy stock and smashed it into the back of Madge's neck. She collapsed in a heap on the ground.

"Bastard," Fargo hissed.

"Now start walking, up the side to the top," Barry said.

"You figure to hold me as a bargaining chip again? Forget it. They won't bargain now. They've won," Fargo said.

"No bargains anymore, you stinkin' bastard," the man snarled. "I just want you far enough away so's they won't hear me shoot you. After that I'll go my way. Until I come back," Barry added ominously.

He prodded Fargo in the back with the gun, and Fargo paused to look down at Madge before he started walking. She was breathing, but it'd be awhile before she woke, and when she did she'd have a very bad headache and a very sore neck. "You've lost, Barry. Give it up," Fargo said.

"I'm still going to win. You have the damn map in your jacket. You haven't had time to tell them about it. They'll go back to their grubby little farms and hog pens, and they still won't know what they're sitting on. I'll hire me another band of gun-slingers, and I'll come back and do what I didn't get to do this time, but you won't be around to get in my way. It'll be even easier because they won't be expecting it."

Fargo swore under his breath. Barry had spelled out a chain of events that were all too workable. The rifle prodded him in the back again, and Fargo hurried his steps. The small ranchers would have had a victory that was only a temporary triumph. Ben Adams and Ellie Willis would remain unavenged. It was bitter, too bitter. He couldn't let it end this way. Yet he had little choice as he felt the rifle barrel push into his back again. He had reached the top of the slope and the land leveled and became a forest of hackberry.

"Keep going. We're still too close," Barry said.

"You know what'll happen when I don't show up back on the cut," Fargo said.

"They'll come looking for you," Barry said.

"They'll find Madge and know something went wrong," Fargo said.

"That'll take awhile. You'll be a dead man by then, and I'll be on my way," Barry said. Once again Fargo cursed silently at the truth in the man's words. The forest grew thicker. It would muffle the sound of a shot, and they were far enough from the cut. He had perhaps another sixty seconds to live, he guessed, and he desperately searched the forest as he slowed his steps. A length of fallen log lay in front of him, and he gathered his muscles. There was no waiting time left. The log was round and wide, and he stepped on top of it and then to the ground. His head turned enough to see. He saw Barry follow, step on the log, and for that split second the rifle barrel pointed aside.

Fargo spun, kicked out with one leg, and hit Barry in the calf at the same time he flung himself backward. The shot whizzed past his head as Barry's leg went out from under him and he fell across the log. But Fargo was at his feet, diving at Joseph Barry as the man tried to bring the rifle around for another shot that went off as Fargo bowled into him. Barry went down partly still on the log, and the gun fell from his hands. Fargo kicked it away as Barry dived for it and missed, rolling across the ground. Fargo slammed into Barry as the man yanked a revolver from his holster and tried to fire point-blank into Fargo's face.

An elbow jammed into Barry's throat made his shot go wild. Fargo rolled with the man and grabbed for the revolver as Barry tried another shot that came dangerously close to his face. But Fargo closed his hand around the man's wrist, bent it backward, and Barry lost his grip on the gun. Barry tried to lunge for it where it lay on the grass, but Fargo wrapped an arm about his throat, yanked him backward, and flung him aside, almost atop the log. Barry rose and swung. Fargo parried the blow and sent his own looping left that landed alongside Barry's head. The man staggered backward and lowered his head and charged.

Fargo brought up a short left and right, and Joseph Barry's head bounced backward. Fargo stepped forward, shot a left hook that sent Barry another step back, and followed with a whistling right cross. It smashed into the point of Barry's jaw so that he arched backward and came down against the log. Fargo heard the cracking sound as Barry's head hit the side of the log. He stepped to the man's still form, knelt down, and moved Barry's head. It fell sideways, his neck broken.

Fargo rose. It was really over now, at last. The

victory that had almost become a silent defeat waiting to be consummated was a victory once again. He wanted to feel better than he did, but there were too many shadows in this triumph. He walked back to the slope, found Madge, and he was gently bringing her around when Orville and Ted Olson appeared. They carried her down, applied a cold canteen to her neck, and then began the trip back to Moon Lake.

"We lost eight," Orville told him. "Cousins and uncles mostly."

Fargo nodded and watched the dead being placed on their horses for the final trip back.

"Let me ride with you," Madge said, and he was happy to agree. She nestled herself against him in the saddle all the way back. When they returned to Moon Lake, he gathered them all and brought out the map.

"Here's why the Barrys wanted you all dead and gone," he said and quickly told them the meaning of the old parchment.

"I'll be damned," Orville said, and Fargo saw Doc Elton standing by. "We're all gonna be rich," Orville said.

"Comfortable if not rich," Fargo said. "You really won't know till you start mining the land."

"I'll have to start charging you all more for my visits," Doc Elton said.

"I'll go to Barry's place and find the old prospector," Fargo said.

"I'll be waiting when you get back," Madge said, and he put the horse into a trot and headed for the Barry ranch. It was a silent place, only the cattle and extra horses in the corrals. He called out Enoch's name and got no answer, and he called again. There was still no answer so he dismounted and walked into the house. Enoch's shirtless, shoeless body lay on the floor, a bullet through the frail chest. Seth or Joseph Barry, Fargo knew at once, before they had left. They didn't want to take the time to put Enoch back in the cell, and they couldn't have him wandering off. He knew too much.

Fargo cursed silently and returned to the Ovaro. That'd be one more to add to the burial. Madge was waiting as she had promised when he returned to her place, and she came to him wearing only a thin, blue cotton dress. His hands told him she'd nothing on underneath. "Maybe you'd consider staying on now that I'm going to be a wealthy woman," she murmured.

His smile was gently chiding and she sniffed.

"Maybe you'd consider staying on awhile now that I'm a passionate woman," she whispered.

"Now you're talking, honey," he said as he slipped the dress from her.

LOOKING FORWARD!

The following is the opening section from the next novel in the exciting *Trailsman* series from Signet:

THE TRAILSMAN #138
SILVER FURY

1860—in a remote region of the Rocky Mountains where the unwary seldom lived long . . .

Someone was following him.

The big man astride the sure-footed pinto stallion did nothing to betray that he was aware of being trailed as he wound his slow way upward along a narrow game trail. Skye Fargo was no stranger to the West; he knew the wild, pristine land better than most, and he knew that those who survived the longest were the ones who never acted rashly. Recklessness was certain suicide, and he aimed to live to a ripe old age and die in bed with a passionate vixen cuddled at his side.

So he kept on riding, sitting loosely in the saddle, his brawny left hand lightly clasping the reins, his lake blue eyes fixed on the pines and aspens lining the trail ahead while his keen ears strained for more telltale sounds from the owl-hoot dogging him. It must be someone up to no good, he reasoned, or whoever it was wouldn't be trying so hard to be stealthy. And failing miserably.

Fargo had heard several twigs snap, and once a small stone rattled down the slope on his left, which told him he wasn't being stalked by Indians. No self-respecting warrior would make so much noise. It was a white man, then, and one with little wilderness experience. Even so, the man must be considered highly dangerous. A bullet from a greenhorn's gun was just as deadly as a slug from the six-shooter of a seasoned *pistolero*.

He figured the unknown stalker had been behind him for better than five minutes. Somehow, he must force the man out into the open. At any moment he might be shot in the back, a thought that caused his skin to prickle. Shifting slightly in the saddle, he casually rested his right hand within inches of his Colt.

The trail brought him to the top of a rise where a wide clearing gave him an excuse to rein up and dismount. Fargo deliberately turned the stallion so that he swung down on the far side from the trees where the stalker was concealed. As his right boot touched the ground, he palmed the Colt and held it between his body and the Ovaro. Then he pretended to adjust the cinch while surreptitiously peering out from under the brim of his white hat at the wall of vegetation below.

Something rustled in a dense thicket.

Fargo glimpsed a flash of color, a streak of blue against the backdrop of green. Then a slim figure in a blue homespun shirt and white-tan cotton duck pants appeared, darting from tree to tree, drawing ever closer. Clutched in the man's hands was a rifle. Fargo was ready to throw himself to either side should the man level the gun, but, oddly enough, the greenhorn didn't bother to bring the weapon into play. Instead, holding the barrel vertical, the man raced to the edge of the clearing and abruptly halted.

"Don't make any sudden moves if you value your life, mister!" he bellowed, his brown eyes ablaze with resolve. An unkempt beard covered the lower half of his angular face.

Fargo straightened and touched the hammer of his Colt. All it would take was a flick of his arm upward, and he could drop the man before the greenhorn knew what was happening, but he held his fire. "Howdy, stranger," he said pleasantly. "What can I do for you?"

He looked to be all tuckered out and as skittish as a colt at a branding. Swallowing, he licked his thin lips, and nodded at the stallion. "I need your horse, mister. If you step back and let me take him, there won't be any trouble." He paused and scanned the forest ringing them. "I'm truly sorry about this, but I have no choice."

"Horse stealing can get a man hanged in these parts," Skye said.

"I'm dead anyway if I don't light a shuck," the man said forlornly and broke into a fit of violent coughing. He was clearly ill. His skin was unnaturally pale, and he appeared to have recently lost a great deal of weight. His shabby clothes, which once must have fit, hung on his scarecrow frame in droopy folds. Both boots had holes in them, and one was missing the heel. He wore no hat. His long black hair, greasy and dishevelled, made him look even more crazy.

"You look like you could use a hot meal and plenty of rest," Fargo commented. "How about if I whip up a pot of fresh coffee?"

Astonishment etched the man's features. "Didn't you hear me?" he demanded, advancing several strides and wagging the rifle. "I need your horse. If you don't get out of the way right this instant, I'm liable to kill you."

"You're not the killing kind."

"What?" the man blurted. "How can you say a thing like that? You don't know me."

"True. But I've run into enough gunmen, renegades, and savages in my time to know a hardened killer when I see one," Fargo said, elevating his arm a bit higher. "If you were really cold-blooded, you would have shot me back on the trail when you were following me."

"You knew I was there?"

"You made more noise than a herd of buffalo," Fargo said. Suddenly he extended his arm over the top of the saddle, trained the Colt on the man's chest, and cocked the hammer. "Now why don't you put down that rifle, and we'll talk this over?"

The man stiffened and made as if to point his rifle. One glance at Fargo's face changed his mind, and he reluctantly lowered the gun to the ground. "Damn me for being the biggest fool in all creation!" he muttered.

"What's your handle?" Fargo asked, being careful to keep the Colt fixed on the greenhorn as he stepped around the stallion.

"Pitman. Charlie Pitman."

"If you don't mind my saying so, Charlie, you'd better rustle up a new line of work. You sure weren't cut out to be an outlaw."

"I'm no thief!" Pitman bristled. "I was a wrangler before I got a fool notion into my head to see some more of the world." He pressed a palm to his sweaty brow. "If I wasn't desperate, I'd never, ever do something like this."

"Care to explain?"

Pitman again surveyed the forest, then said nervously, "Gladly, mister. But first we have to hightail it out of here before they show up."

"They?"

"The bastards who are out for my hide. They don't take kindly to someone escaping, and they'll track me down for sure. That Cutler can follow a fox over solid rock, they say."

His curiosity fully aroused, Fargo walked over to pick up Pitman's rifle, then mounted the Ovaro and motioned at the sea of trees to the south of the clearing. "Lead the way. I'll tell you when to stop." He saw relief on the man's face as Pitman turned and entered the cover of the woods. There could be no doubt that Pitman was genuinely scared to death of whoever was after him. Who could it be? And why?

They traveled twenty yards before the scarecrow spoke. "If I make it out of this mess alive, I swear that I'm going back to Ohio and visit my folks. I never should have left home five years ago in the first place."

An irate squirrel, upset by their intrusion into its domain, chattered angrily at them from a high limb.

"Sometimes a fella doesn't realize how good he has things until he loses them," Pitman went on. "If I'd known what was in store for me when I rode off, I'd have stayed put." Once more he mopped his forehead. "But I was younger then. I figured I knew it all. Went to Texas and got me a job on a ranch. It was all right for a spell. Wrangling is hard work, though, and it wears a man down after a while. So I took my pay and headed for Denver. There, I got me the idea to go to California." Pitman snorted. "What a jackass!"

Fargo had met many such men in his travels, roamers filled with an unquenchable wanderlust, carefree souls eager to see the many wonders the country had to offer. They drifted from place to place, job to job, always seeking something better over the next horizon. Why there were so many was no great secret. The lure of adventure the untamed land west of the Mississippi River promised drew them like a magnet attracted bits of iron. They could no more resist the call of the wild than they could stop breathing—as he well knew, because he shared their urge to see all there was to see.

As Pitman began relating his childhood in Ohio, Fargo listened with half an ear. The rest of his attention was focused on the sounds and rhythms of the forest. He heard sparrows singing gaily off to the right and the breeze rustling through the pines.

The squirrel chattered for a minute, then abruptly ceased.

"—Pa always wanted me to follow in his footsteps and be a farmer," Pitman was saying. "But no! I was too good for that kind of work. You wouldn't catch me plowing a field or feeding slop to a bunch of hungry hogs!" He laughed bitterly. "I thought the life of a farmer was the most boring life in the world. I wanted something better."

"Did you find it?" Fargo asked.

"I sure as hell did not," Pitman said. "Instead I learned that farming is no worse than most other jobs. In fact, it's better. No matter what a man does for a living, he has to work hard at it if he wants to make something of himself."

For over a hundred yards they moved in silence except for the dull clumping of the Ovaro's hoofs.

"Tell me more about these people who are after you," Fargo prompted. He had heard nothing to indicate there was anyone else within miles of where they were, but he still believed the man's story and wanted to learn as much as he could about the situation before anyone showed up.

"When we stop," Pitman said.

The soft gurgling of water drew them to a grassy tract flanking a gently flowing stream. Pitman immediately sank to his knees and gulped greedily, getting his chin and shirt soaking wet. "Lord, this hits the spot! I haven't had a drop to drink since I ran off. That was pretty near twenty-four hours ago."

Fargo wedged the man's rifle into his bedroll, then climbed down and let the stallion drink its fill.

He studied his newfound acquaintance, noting the deep lines in Pitman's haggard face and the flecks of gray in the man's greasy hair. Pitman looked to be thirty-five or forty, but Fargo had the impression he was much younger. "If you don't mind my asking, Charlie, how old are you?"

Pitman paused in the act of scooping more water to his mouth. "Twenty-four, but you'd never guess it from the way I look. That's what they did to me. Nine months at hard labor is enough to ruin any man."

"Hard labor?" Fargo repeated. "Were you in prison?"

Pitman looked up and opened his mouth to answer when the stillness around them was shattered by the harsh blast of a gun. At that moment the center of Pitman's forehead burst outward as a slug tore through his head from back to front, showering blood, flesh, and gore all over the grass. Charlie uttered a strangled groan and pitched forward.

Fargo was in motion before the echo of the blast died away. Automatically pinpointing the direction the shot came from, he crouched and whirled toward the undergrowth where the rifleman lurked, his Colt flashing from its holster. He saw telltale wisps of gunsmoke thirty yards away above dense brush on the other side of the stream and fired three times in swift succession, fanning the revolver and elevating the barrel a hair to compensate for the range. Then he lunged at the stallion, grabbed the reins, and pulled the pinto into cover behind some pines. In a twinkling he had his Sharps in his hand and the Colt back on his hip.

An eerie quiet enveloped the forest. All the birds and other wildlife had fallen mute.

Fargo leaned against a trunk and fed a bullet into the Sharps. He glanced once at Charlie Pitman, sprawled limply on the dank earth with a crimson pool forming around his head, before moving on cat's feet toward the water. Had he hit the bushwhacker? Or was the man just waiting out there for the chance to slay him, too?

At the last pine fronting the stream he stopped to scour the forest beyond and to gird himself for the next step. He had to cross a narrow strip of grass, vault the stream, and reach the trees beyond. For three or four seconds he would be in the open, exposed and helpless.

Taking a deep breath, Fargo hurtled from behind the trunk, darted to the bank, and leaped. To the southwest a rifle cracked and something nipped at the fringe adorning the left side of his buckskins. Then he landed solidly on both soles, ducked down, and scooted into a tangle of bushes.

Fargo flattened himself and aimed his rifle. There were two triggers on a Sharps: by pulling the rear one, Fargo set the front trigger so that all he had to do was tap it and the rifle would fire. Such a hair trigger came in handy when a man had to shoot in a hurry, when the difference between life and death could be measured in the blink of an eye.

Rising but staying hunched over, he angled to the right. The rifleman had prudently changed position, moving ten yards to the north of where he had been when he shot Pitman. This was no greenhorn.

Something told Fargo that he was up against someone skilled at killing.

He used every available cover, his eyes constantly sweeping back and forth, alert for any movement. Whoever was out there was bound to move again and might give himself away. Skirting a thicket, he glided to a fir tree and stopped to get his bearings.

Once more the crisp mountain air shattered in the boom of a large-caliber rifle.

The trunk next to Fargo's cheek exploded in a shower of splinters and bits of woods. Instinctively he dropped down, then sprinted for a large boulder a dozen feet away. Taking a flying dive, he landed on his elbows and knees, brutally jarring his limbs.

His pulse pounded like a tom-tom. That had been too damn close for comfort! he reflected, and rose to his knees. He touched his left hand to his cheek, and when he lowered the hand there were drops of blood on the tips of his first two fingers. If one of those razor-sharp slivers had struck an eye, he'd have been blinded.

The rifleman had changed position again. This time the shot had come from a point fifteen yards to the left of where the killer had been positioned when he fired as Fargo jumped the stream. Fargo knew the man was probably moving once more at that very moment. But which way? If he could outguess the bastard, he'd turn the tables.

He risked a peek over the boulder and nearly lost his head. Stone chips stung his face as a slug scored a groove close to the tip of his nose, then ricocheted off into the vegetation. Going prone, he crawled into high weeds to his rear, slanted to the left, and snaked his way in a loop intended to bring him up on the bushwhacker from the rear.

Suddenly he spotted a vague shape jogging in a beeline to the north. There was a hint of buckskins, and he glimpsed some sort of fur cap. Whipping the Sharps to his shoulder, he took a hasty bead, steadied the barrel, and squeezed off a shot.

The man disappeared.

Had he missed? Fargo wondered, hastily inserting a new cartridge. He remembered to move, to put himself somewhere else in case the bushwhacker had pinpointed where he was, and galvanized into motion, sprinting to the right. It was well he did. A fraction of a second after he took his first step, a bullet buzzed through the very space his body had just occupied.

The killer was very much alive.

Fargo plunged into shoulder-high brush, plowed a path into the center, and abruptly halted, crouching to catch his wind. Faintly he heard pounding footsteps, then silence. The rifleman had moved again—but where?

Lowering onto his stomach, Fargo removed his hat and held it in his left hand as he swiftly crawled to the west edge of the brush. Dappled by shadows and sparkling beams of sunlight, the forest presented a deceptive picture of tranquility. He searched high and low but saw no sign of the killer. Putting his hat back on, he braced his left hand on the ground and tensed to shove erect when out of the corner of his left eye he spied a bright glimmer of light, the reflection of sunlight off a metal gun barrel.

Fargo frantically threw himself to the right. He heard the killer's rifle thunder and felt dirt strike his face as the bullet smacked into the soil. Twisting, he hastily sighted on the tree shielding the mystery rifleman and fired, doubting he would score but hoping to give the killer pause long enough for him to reach safety.

Springing up, Fargo ran to a spruce and ducked behind the bole. Another shot blasted, the slug thudding into the trunk. Hunkering down, he fed a fresh cartridge into the Sharps, cocked the hammer, and set the trigger. So far he had been incredibly lucky, but he couldn't expect his luck to last forever. Either he figured a way to end the fight and end it quickly, or he'd wind up like Charlie Pitman.

Fargo had to hand it to the killer. The man was as good as they came, as good as *he* was, even, an equal—someone with as much experience as he had, someone whose skill set him apart from the ordinary frontiersman. Such men were not all that common. Kit Carson, Jim Bridger, Joe Walker, and a dozen or so others were equally renowned, but they were men of great personal integrity, not the kind to shoot someone from ambush. The man he was up against had to be a scout or mountain man gone bad.

Fargo had met most of the more famous frontiersmen at one time or another. And those he hadn't met, he'd heard about. Small wonder, since the favorite pastime in every saloon and tavern in the settlements and around every campfire on the Oregon Trail and other routes west was the sharing of the latest news concerning the exploits of men who deservedly earned widespread reputations. Intrepid explorers like Bridger and Walker and adventurers like Carson were household names.

So, too, was the name of the Trailsman, though Fargo had never asked for the title. Somewhere along the line someone came up with it and the name stuck. Now, wherever he went, that was how he was known. Not that he minded. Troublemakers were less inclined to tangle with someone rumored to eat live grizzlies for breakfast.

Now, as Fargo scanned the woods on all sides, he wondered if he knew the man trying to kill him or whether he had heard the man spoken of at one time or another. The odds were he had. It made no difference, though. He would shoot the son of a bitch dead the minute he got a clear shot, and that would be that.

A minute passed. Two. Vigilant as a hawk, Fargo scrutinized every shadow, surveyed every possible hiding place, but spied no one. Immobile, he waited for the killer to make a mistake, but the man never did. After five minutes of absolute quiet, he took a gamble. Squatting, he picked up a small stone, then threw it with all his might.

The stone struck a fir tree and clattered to the earth.

Fargo had the Sharps tucked to his shoulder, ready to fire. But there was no reaction from the killer. The man didn't fall for the ploy and snap off a shot in the direction of the sound, as Fargo had hoped. Perhaps the killer was gone, he speculated. Yet it wouldn't do to step out into the open, not until he was certain.

For ten more minutes he stayed where he was. Finally several sparrows flitted through the trees across the way, singing merrily as they frolicked. A jay, betraying no alarm, alighted in a nearby pine. He saw a butterfly fluttering through the undergrowth. The wild creatures were resuming their interrupted lives, which meant all was well.

Still, Fargo proceeded cautiously. He conducted a search of the area and found clear tracks in the soft soil at the base of a tree. They were moccasin prints, and they revealed the killer to weigh two hundred pounds or better judging by their depth. Working outward from the tree, he found where the man had run off, going to the east.

Giving chase would be pointless. The killer had a five- to ten-minute head start and must be a mile off already. More, if the man had a horse hidden nearby.

Fargo contented himself with examining the ground for more footprints. A competent tracker could tell a lot about a person from the tracks the person made. In this case, based on the way the killer had moved with his toes pointed slightly inward, Fargo deduced the bushwhacker might be part Indian because white men invariably walked with their toes pointed outward.

Fargo's hunch was confirmed by the shape of the tracks themselves. No two Indian tribes made their moccasins the same way; the shapes of the heels and the toes were always unique with each one. The Crows, for instance, wore moccasins that curved from the heel to the toe. Pawnees wore moccasins with exceptionally wide soles. Kiowas preferred moccasins sporting narrow toes.

The tracks he found bore slender heels and wide toes. Those were the earmarks of Arapaho moccasins. So it was possible the killer had spent a lot of time with that tribe. He straightened, his brow knit in thought. A fuzzy recollection nipped at the back of his mind, something he had heard once about a mountain man living with the Arapahos, but he couldn't remember the whole story.

Shrugging, Fargo headed for the stream. He would have to bury Pitman. Then what? Should he press on westward as he had been doing when the greenhorn appeared, or should he try to track down the killer? Unable to decide, he waded the shallow water and walked past Pitman's corpse. At the pines beyond he stopped, rage flaring within him.

The Ovaro was gone.